P E N G U I N · S H O R T · F I C T I O N

"Not that the story need be long, but it will take a long while to make it short."

— Henry David Thoreau

Treasure Island

Jean Howarth was born in Kelwood, Manitoba, and grew up in a series of small prairie communities where her father served as minister. She has worked for *The Calgary Herald*, CBC radio and *The Vancouver Province*. Jean was introduced to Saturna Island by poet Earle Birney, and her columns in *The Globe and Mail* about her Treasure Island have attracted a loyal readership.

TREASURE ISLAND

Jean Howarth

Penguin Books

Penguin Books Canada Ltd., 2801 John Street, Markham, Ontario, Canada L3R 1B4
Penguin Books Ltd., Harmondsworth, Middlesex, England
Penguin Books, 40 West 23rd Street, New York
Penguin Books Australia Ltd., Ringwood, Victoria, Australia
Penguin Books (N.Z.) Ltd., 182-190 Wairau Road, Auckland 10, New Zealand

First published by Dorset Publishing Inc., 1979

Published in Penguin Books, 1984

Copyright © Jean Howarth, 1979
All rights reserved

Manufactured in Canada by Webcom.

*All the characters in this book are fictitious, and any
resemblance to actual persons living or dead is coincidental*

Canadian Cataloguing in Publication Data

Howarth, Jean.
Treasure Island

A collection of columns which first appeared in the Globe and Mail.
ISBN 0-14-007066-4

I. The Globe and mail. II. Title.

PS8565.0875T74 1984   C818'.5408   C83-098793-2
PR9199.3.H683T74 1984

To Richard J. Doyle,
the best editor in Canada,
who named Treasure Island and insisted on
carrying it on the editorial page of
The Globe & Mail,
even though some staffers
felt it rather lowered the tone.

and

To Jim and Lou Money,
the seigniors of
the manor.

W HAT this country needs is a place to get away from itself. We have therefore decided to give you honorary admission to our island. It is off the coast and it is called Madronna.

Excitement on Madronna centers at the moment around the graveyard. The islanders decided they needed their own graveyard when an elderly islander died and after they had settled up his affairs and paid mainland funeral costs, there was only $38.21 left to send to his daughter in New Brunswick whom he hadn't seen for 38 years.

The Community Club bought the graveyard from the mainland School Board for $1. (It had been the schoolyard until a forest fire took out the school but left the teacherage. The new school is on the waterfront where the volunteer fire brigade can put water on it from the sea.) The islanders are turning the teacherage into a chapel, and one of their summer visitors who is a surveyor has surveyed the old schoolyard into cemetery plots.

Captain O'Grady got the first plot. He claims he has his captain's papers from the Port of London but he hasn't. He just stole a yachting cap from a visiting yacht. He got the first plot by asking Postmaster Jim Carpenter, who is also the storekeeper, for a pouch of snuff. While Jim went round the partition that divides the post office from the store, the Cap stole the letter addressed to the Community Club containing the survey.

He returned it to Jim Carpenter that night, marked "opened by mistake," and put in for a plot by the gate in the fence which the islanders are building around the cemetery. The Cap likes to see what is going on. He did not pay the $5 which is the cost of a plot in Madronna cemetery. Jim Carpenter agreed to take it out of the sale of the captain's outboard motor (also stolen from a visiting yacht) after the Cap dies.

Other residents have since staked their claims. Hobart Coyne and Bert Walshe have taken adjoining plots. They play crib most nights and plan to continue the game underground. Dan Potter took a double plot for himself and his wife under a large maple tree. Dan is the meanest man on Madronna. He won't let anybody use his beach even though it isn't his beach but the public's. People who tie their boats to his float find them going out on the next tide, and the last picnickers got a hornets' nest in their midst. Of course the hornets stung Dan too, but that was all right. Dan doesn't even like Dan.

He picked the spot under the maple because the digging there will be hard.

Old Mildred Stonehenge has dug a posthole for the cemetery fence for each one of her 91 years. She used the posthole digger she made herself.

Grandpa Cuthbert, who is 89, tottered down on his son's arm to pick out his last resting place. Right at the back, where he can keep an eye on the rest of us. Old Mrs. Stonehenge and Grandpa Cuthbert are gripped in a double-edged rivalry. Each intends to outlive the other, but each intends to be the first islander into the new cemetery.

It has left them both spending much time hoping that the other will be lost at sea.

THE way the site for the first Madronna Island school was picked was what Mrs. Carpenter and Mrs. Cuthbert called participatory democracy, and what the Dansons, the Robertsons and the Bateses called a damned outrage.

The four island families with schoolage children lived at the four corners of the island. The four mothers were tired of giving correspondence courses, and because there were now nine children the mainland school board had agreed to put up a one-room school and pay a teacher. But each family wanted the school in its own cove.

After a particularly passionate meeting of the Community Club, it was decided that a parent from each family, compass in hand, would start out at nine a.m. (watches synchronized and the rest of the islanders acting as referees) and walk toward the middle of the island. Where they met they would build the school.

The Dansons, the Robertsons and the Bateses were represented by male parents, who made the mistake of treating the event as a walking contest. The Cuthberts, coached by Mrs. Carpenter, were represented by Mrs. Cuthbert, who kept getting thorns in her shoes and was a very slow mountain climber. By the time they met, the Cuthbert contingent had managed only one mountain while the male striders from the other families had all managed two.

The Dansons, the Robertsons and the Bateses demanded a rewalk. But Mr. Carpenter, who is great on justice, said that the same opportunities had been available to all and that if they didn't start building the school soon it would be back to correspondence courses. Mrs. Carpenter, who had not confided her strategy to Mr. Carpenter, said she couldn't help it if men were boneheads.

Actually, it was a pleasant place for a school, give or take a mountain or two. A nice level glade for the school-house, schoolyard and teacherage. A brook wandering down from one of the mountains to make a small marsh, replete with bull frogs and bulrushes. The school and teacherage went up in no time, and that September Mrs. Gathercole, the teacher, opened Madronna's first school with 10 children—she'd brought along one of her own.

In October, unfortunately, a forest fire roared down from one of the mountains. When the frantic island fought through with bulldozers to the school they found it gone, the teacherage unaccountably still standing and the island's young preserved by Mrs. Gathercole who had got them all down in the marsh with wet blankets over their heads.

After that they put the school where Mrs. Carpenter said it should have been all along, at the head of our deepest bay, June Harbor. True, the building had originally been a chicken house. But the men lined it with rough lumber from the island's sawmill and the women used lysol.

If one has to go to school, it isn't a bad place The sea is there, for swimming and finding big eating crabs among the seaweed when the tide is out. Ospreys dive for salmon. A family of raccoons comes along at lunch time for hand-outs. And the crows have taught the children not to leave their lunch buckets on the porch. A good crow can open a lunch bucket in 30 seconds.

And since the mainland school board is—no other word for it—stingy, Mrs. Gathercole has the children growing mushrooms in the basement to sell in Mr. Carpenter's store. With the proceeds they will buy a baseball, a bat, and a crab trap.

The chickens seem to have left their successors quite a rich heritage.

4

WE knew about the accident, of course. It was on the radio, and the Falkners had come to Madronna every summer—four kids and the mother and dad. All wiped out in one collision except nine-year-old Ronnie and his five-year-old sister, Penny, who'd been locked up together in a seat belt.

We were sorry and made a funeral wreath. But we were startled when Ronnie came down the gangway of the weekly boat about a month later, leading Penny by the hand.

He looked like a little old man, hanging onto Penny—she's retarded—as though they were welded together. He went unseeing through the rest of us and stopped in front of the six-foot-four that is Mr. Carpenter. "Could we talk to you, Mister?" he asked.

Mr. Carpenter, who is postmaster and storekeeper and road foreman and justice of the peace, abandoned these duties and took the two children up to his house in behind the store. That night he summoned us to an emergency meeting of the Community Club. "It's those Falkner kids," he said when we arrived. "Mary Jo's got them upstairs so they can't hear us. But we've got to work fast."

Ronnie and Penny, he explained, had been left without relatives, only each other, and the children's aid proposed to send Penny to a home for the retarded and Ronnie to a foster home.

"Ronnie won't have it," he said. "What we've got to do is find a foster home for the pair of them here on Madronna. Before the children's aid gets the police out after them. And then I'll call Milt Foster and put the arm on him." Milt Foster is an eminent mainland lawyer who once got his powerboat on a reef. Charlie Jo, passing in the family boat, picked him off and revived him with some of Captain O'Grady's home-distilled gin, and the rest of Madronna went out and salvaged his boat.

Three island families offered to take the children. We talked it over. It was felt that the Tuckers' offer would have to be dismissed, because the Tuckers are common-lawing and the children's aid wouldn't like it. The Welches wouldn't do either, because they have an outhouse and no running water and the children's aid would object to that. But the Davises were suitable. They are married and have an indoor toilet and Flo Davis has a good tweed suit with a skirt. The children's aid couldn't possibly object.

"Yes, they could," said Mrs. Carpenter. "They'll say this island is too remote and ignorant and hasn't got television. Remember the time they tried to keep Jill Bates from adopting her second until we got that newspaper man to tell on them. I think we should call him right away."

"Later," said Mr. Carpenter, "if the law doesn't work." And he went to the phone to call Milt Foster.

He told him all about it. The accident. The two children seeing it and surviving it and having nobody left but each other. And the children's aid set on serving-the-good-of-the-child by separating them.

"Young Ronnie," he explained, "just stole some money from the group home where they are now and lit out for here. He'll do anything to keep his sister with him. And there's a good, respectable family that will take them. You've got to fix it.

"Young Ronnie," he told Milt Foster, "says he will work for their keep. He says he'll cut kindling and carry in wood and spade the garden next spring. He says the little girl can help too. He says she's just a little retarded. He says she can wash the supper dishes, if we'll let her stand on a chair so the water won't run down her elbows and make a puddle on the floor."

ON Madronna we know how the heathen felt about missionaries.

We were busy turning the teacherage at the old school site into a chapel. Jed Peterson, who used to be a carpenter in Sussex, had built a pulpit and was making a stand-by coffin with the help of Charlie Jo. The coffin is the old-fashioned kind, narrow at the feet, broadening for the shoulders and curving around the head. The wood has to be steamed to take the curve, and that's done more easily by two. Besides, Jed wanted Charlie to learn the rudiments. Charlie might be building the next coffin for Jed.

The less skilled were making cedar pews for the congregation and relaying the floor. Since we do not have electric power on Madronna it was taking a lot of hand-sanding.

Almost everybody except infants and Captain O'Grady was involved in the project.

At which point Captain O'Grady, who avoids all work when possible but is a wonder at gleaning gossip, turned up to announce that we needn't bother. The Bishop had persuaded his former parish in Toronto to give the poor benighted people of Madronna a church. He'd bought the land, and a crew to put up the pre-fabricated church would be arriving next week.

We didn't believe him. With reason. We didn't know we had a Bishop. We didn't know that somebody had put us in his parish. We hadn't asked anybody for a church. What we wanted was a chapel. All sects welcome.

It was true, though.

The crew arrived the next week. They put up the church in five days—"Even the Lord," said Mr. Carpenter, our justice of the peace, "would have taken six"—and out-

7

fitted it with real pews and a real pulpit. Perhaps the worst insult was that the kneelers—the Bishop's parishioners kneel to pray—were cushioned, and the cushions had been covered with hand-made needlepoint.

We could just see those Toronto characters needle-pointing for our souls.

The Bishop is coming on Sunday to consecrate his church.

It makes a real problem. Not only that we are all in a smoulder of rage against the far-away smugness that has condescended to us. But we have our culture and traditions, and one of them is being hospitable to strangers, even Bishops.

Mr. Carpenter is leading the half of the island that will break with tradition and not be in the church on Sunday.

Mrs. Carpenter is leading the half of the island that will turn the other cheek. In addition she wishes to see the inside of THAT BUILDING and examine THOSE KNEELERS with her own eyes.

Perhaps the most practical response has been that of Charlie Jo. Being an Indian he was able to put out a rush call through the Indian fishing fleet for an up-coast evangelist who came and baptized the entire junior population, from Charlie down, in Clare Creek. The Bishop's church has a baptismal font.

When the Bishop arrives on Sunday he may find us poor. We do not feel poor but he is entitled to his opinion.

But he sure as hell won't find us benighted.

WHEN the eagles fly home at night you can hear their wings. I can testify to this of my own knowledge. We were sitting—the kids and I—on the cliffside under our house looking out to the sea. Not talking, because we were counting under our breath to see how long it would be before a ship could be heard coming round Joshua Point or Bergan Head. The sky was that pale gold after the sun has gone.

These two eagles flew over our heads. Together, rather companionably, which is a little unusual for eagles. And we could hear the dip, dip, dip of their wings.

The peace of an island.

Well, not exactly.

There is a kind of quiet, in that all the city sounds are absent. No traffic, no hum of human activity. Sometimes this absence of the usual sounds sends city dwellers into a panic and onto Syd Kenney's small boat ($1 for adults, 50 cents for children) to catch the next ship back to the city from one of the more urban islands.

But there are country noises. Raccoons squabbling at night in the fruit trees can sound like a barroom brawl. And maybe it is. They throw things, and once two of them got so concentrated on the hand-to-hand combat that they forgot they were up a tree and fell out. No damage. They just picked themselves up and went on with the fight. In the fall they compete with us for the produce of our orchards and berry patches, taking the fruit just on the green side, if possible the night before they think we'll take it. They try to outguess us, as we try to outguess them. But in an abandoned orchard, over at Brinker cove, they let the fruit ripen and fall and ferment, and then they tie one on. If you sneak up and lie in the bushes on the edge of the orchard, there is no question of its being a barroom brawl. Country noise.

An owl hooting outside your bedroom window can sound like doom serving notice, though if you catch him in the beam of a flashlight he may be no taller than 10 inches.

Tree frogs sound like a base fiddle, plucked slowly.

The carpenter ants in one wall of the house sound, after bedtime, like the crackle of a fire. When we had a visiting fireman once—a real fireman, visiting, I mean—he could handle the ants until he dropped into that place between sleep and waking when dreams become reality, and then he would think it was a real fire and come roaring out to save us all.

After the third eruption, the adults gave it up and spent the rest of the night playing poker. And the next night we made him take his sleeping bag to a cave in the cliff.

As for the squirrel in our attic counting his acorns, he sounds like God playing bowls.

No, not exactly quiet.

Especially if you count the ships. And it takes a strong mind not to count them. They come in-bound around Joshua Point and out-bound around Bergan Head, and the throb of their engines can be heard long before they come into view. If the foghorn isn't bawling, that is.

We had a Saskatchewan farm visitor one week. After suffering through a night of the foghorn, she appeared at the breakfast table looking worn. "Will nobody," she asked at large, "take that cow to a bull?"

Many citizens of the urban world have lost track of the connection between eggs and chickens, and few of them would drink milk if they knew anything about the indelicacy of its production. As for outdoor toilets...

Adults are one thing. They adjust or go home. But you can hurt a child badly by letting him see basic things in the wrong way. There's a city boy who has never touched chicken since he saw Mrs. Cuthbert cleaning one. He has a fried egg instead.

Now, when a mainland family first arrives, we borrow Johnny Cuthbert. His mother is always glad to lend him. Even after 12 years of him, she can never be sure what he'll do next except that she'll have to smack him for it.

The thing about Johnny is that he leads and the little urban innocents wouldn't dare not to follow. Usually we see that he starts them off at the evening milking, up at the Carpenters', where Irwin Hoffstater is the milkman. Irwin feeds the cats first. There are three of them. They line up behind the cow as he settles on his milking stool, and he squirts milk into their mouths between the cow's hind legs. When Johnny is there he also squirts milk into Johnny's mouth. The innocents naturally beg to be squirted too. Johnny takes over the second cow. He and Irwin squirt each other. It's a bull's eye when they hit each other's mouths simultaneously. They both squirt the innocents, with Johnny explaining that they have to open their mouths real wide if he's gonna hit their tonsils.

Only about half the milk ends up in the milk pails but Irwin and the Carpenters don't mind. They only took the cows because they're old and they like them and the Cuthberts were going to butcher them.

The innocents come home sopping to report nothing

more alarming than that fresh milk is warm. Funny, huh?

Johnny has a black hen who will almost always lay an egg if he gives her a bit of licorice root and then holds her up and shakes her. An urbanite who catches the egg gets to keep it.

Johnny can always fetch the Cuthbert Clydesdale, Jenny, with a whistle and a hand full of oats—hand flat, you there! my horse don't bite kids but can she help it if you stick your fingers down her throat? Jenny can mount six kids at a time, standing patiently by the fence. She is so big their legs stick straight out either side.

Johnny handles the outdoor toilet problem directly by locking his guests in it one at a time and leaving them there until he hears they done it. If they are not near the amenities he will holler, "Use the bushes!" and shortly after, "Use leaves!" He has had to be instructed not to direct newcomers among the nettles or the poison ivy. It is not that Johnny is disobedient, only that he can think of things to do faster than you can think to tell him not to.

Johnny is always being invited for weekends in town. One minute after he met his first escalator he was riding down the bannister. Ya just lay flat on your stomach and balance with your arms and legs. Some of the urbanites who followed him did not balance so well and were captured by store security. Johnny didn't notice because he was going back up the escalator the wrong way. His hosts of the moment didn't notice (they were in the cafeteria and thought he'd gone to the washroom) until he turned up with the cashier on his tail. He'd found you could get three glasses of milk from the milk spigot for the price of one by drinking two on the spot.

~~~~~~

THE secret of making a government grant serve the community, says Charlie Jo, is knowing your local resources. In this case Jarge Gallagher's dredge, his feeling for Madronna's island neighbor, Cooper, a good supply of raccoons, and the weekly community card party.

Charlie Jo, backed by the Madronna Community Club, negotiated a government grant to pay the wages of himself and six other unemployed teen-agers while they restored Clare Creek as a salmon-spawning stream.

Cleaning Clare Creek consisted of removing the deadfalls and debris with which the loggers had cluttered it, causing silting. But if the salmon were to spawn they needed the clean gravel under the silt, and to reach it Charlie needed a dredge.

Jarge Gallagher maintains a home for old machinery over on the channel side, and as a general rule he rejects pulling his machines out of retirement. "They've done their work, they're entitled to their rest," he will explain to people trying to rent his bulldozer, his piledriver. But Jarge has a large contempt for the island of Cooper because it is richer than Madronna, has a good conceit of itself, and boasts that it has no raccoons—which it hasn't, because of unusually strong currents that have kept them off.

Jarge made a deal with Charlie Jo to dredge Clare Creek if Charlie would supply him with coons to transport to Cooper.

While clearing the creek of deadfalls, the crew had become familiar and shared their lunches with a family of coons—father, mother, three kits. But as Charlie said, "We *know* these coons." So the crew set up live traps on the other side of the mountain to capture strange coons.

The following morning one trap yielded a family of strange coons—father, mother, two kits—and the other traps four adult coons. This presented the crew with an appalling decision they had not anticipated.

If they turned the four adult coons over to Jarge for transporting, how many kits were they leaving to probable starvation on Madronna? One of the co-workers (male) was in favor of trying again for a second family. No, said another co-worker (female); they all knew the dredge had to do its job that night, and no coons for Jarge, no dredge. Well then, said Charlie, they had to decide what was the worst possible thing they could do, and not do it. After much shouting and a few blows, they decided that the worst thing would be to leave unknown kits to starve.

So they let the four adult coons go, and took the family and an empty live trap down to Clare Creek. They had to turn their Judas faces aside as their own family of coons walked trustingly into the live trap to consume the crew's entire lunch. Even coons would not willingly swap Madronna for Cooper.

That night, after eight o'clock, Jarge came round the point with his dredge and dredged Clare Creek, clearing away the silt and leaving the rocks and gravel clean for next autumn's spawning salmon. When it was good and dark he took Madronna's offering of two coon families to a secluded cove on Cooper. Two coon families could populate the world, let alone a second-rate island like Cooper.

The dredging did not take place until after eight o'clock because the government grant crew knew that by that hour all the owners of property fronting on Clare Creek would be at the community hall for the weekly card party. The owners had not been asked if they wanted tons of smelly Clare Creek muck dumped in their front yards.

L ENA Masterson's kitchen is very usefully placed for the benefit of the island. It is on the seaward side of the lighthouse and overlooks the only three bays on the island that can give a boat safe harborage. If Lena does not see the RCMP launch approaching, she hears it.

She goes immediately to the shed that houses the foghorn, starts up the diesel engine that powers it and lets the horn blow through its cycle twice. If she were merely testing the foghorn, she would let it blow five times.

Everybody on the island hears the horn and takes warning.

The men who have colored gas in their cars drain it and replace it with white. The colored gas is taxed 32 cents a gallon less than white, and is supposed to be used only in fishing boats and farm machines.

If the men do not have current licence plates on their trucks they move them on their own land and prepare to swear convincingly to Sergeant Munro that they have never left it. Actually, Mr. Carpenter is the only one who never uses colored gas in his truck and always has current licence plates. As the government road foreman, the postmaster and the justice of the peace, he is a little handicapped for the minor forms of dishonesty. Besides, it is he who will have to drive Sergeant Munro around the island.

The women take the shot-out-of-season sides of venison from their meat houses, wrap them in heavy plastic and store them in the root-cellars in their gardens. That's where we usually keep our extra stocks of Captain O'Grady's gin, too. It is fairly safely stored in old gallon bleach bottles. Two or three under the kitchen sink would not excite curiosity, but the Sergeant would have to take

15

official notice if he saw 30 or 40 of them lined up. We have to keep supplies ahead, because it is never possible to tell when the Captain will be caught stealing something on the mainland and sent to jail. Here at home, Mr. Carpenter looks after him; but the Captain will stray.

If the Captain is down the mine shaft making gin, he turns the still off and goes along to his boat. The still vents itself harmlessly on the far side of the mountain, but Mr. Carpenter has insisted that no chances be taken.

If the Captain is down in Beachcomber's Bay cutting the brand marks off stolen logs, he hides his power saw (also stolen) in a nearby cave. Then it could be anybody who stole the logs and saw, for the Captain always wears gloves when he is about these chores.

By this time it is safe for Mr. Carpenter to go down to the government wharf and catch the ropes of Sergeant Munro's launch and invite him up for lunch.

Today it will be his favorite lunch, island oysters with cheese baked on the half shell, because Mrs. Carpenter knows what he doesn't, that he is in for a nasty job.

That bitch Elinor Filibruster got these two doberman pinschers for status symbols. She has starved them until they are skin and bones and paralyzed in the hind quarters. Old Mildred Stonehenge would have shot them for her, but Elinor demanded the police. So the Sergeant will have to do it.

After he does he will go round behind the Filibruster woodshed and be sick. He can't stand cruelty.

LESTER Cholmondeley is very down on the Government about inflation. It has meant he will have to keep his mink trapline running until the end of the month. "And I never before," says Lester, "had to work past the middle of February."

Lester is against work. He meets his cash needs by snaring wild mink around the coast of Madronna Island. "A mean beast, the mink," he told me. "You should see the throats he slits for the like of it; I could never have used the otter so. And he's a stable beast, too. Riding up and down with the cost of living, as she goes. But now this Government's fixing to force me on the old-age pension." Lester was gloomy. He must be over 70, but his principles forbid application for public aid, even when everyone's doing it.

His cash needs are small. Last year, $246.11. For coal oil and wicks for his lamp. Tea, salt, flour. A side of pork from Eli Cuthbert. Fishing gear. Garden seeds. Shells for his gun ("There's venison and grouse to be shot, but I only"—with virtue—"hunt for the pot"). And his clothes and boots ("though I'm not needing to replace them once in five years.")

No soap. Lester is also against soap. Soap, like work, was one of the Lord's mistakes in the Garden of Eden.

For the rest, he produces his own, and that is not work but pleasure.

There is his garden. His orchard, with all manner of apple trees, cherry trees, pear trees, peach trees, nut trees, even a fig tree. There are his bantam chickens in the trees ("A hardy strain, Missus. I could not have one that would make work. They fend for themselves, and I lay they're so smart the coons never get but two or three of the young ones"). There are mushrooms in the meadow, wild honey in the forest, salmon and herring and cod and halibut in the sea. He cuts his own wood ("And that's an easy thing, with the loggers leaving so much small stuff felled it's a man's duty not to waste"). He makes his own porridge meal from patches of wheat he grows himself. He smokes his own bacon and oysters. He steals his milk from Mrs. Cuthbert's cows.

We had our chat over mugs of Lester's homemade blackberry wine. In Lester's shack you always accept wine over the proffered tea. The alcohol kills the germs.

That night I took Lester's problem to the island's problem center, where Mr. and Mrs. Carpenter run the store, post office and justice of the peace (who is Mr. Carpenter, frequently run by Mrs. Carpenter).

"Yes," said Mr. Carpenter sadly, "I'll have to write the Government about his pension."

"Not yet," said Mrs. Carpenter. "Charlie Jo would help him with his snares. And you can trade him boots and tea and fishing gear for a keg of his wine. The man has his principles. Not," she added darkly, "that you'd often notice. When I think of that poor wife of his!"

"She was a weak thing," said Mr. Carpenter, "not up to the rough ways of the island."

"She was a martyr to that man's laziness," said Mrs. Carpenter. "He wouldn't leave his mink snares out for an extra week, though she and the child were in the worst way for clothes."

"She took the child and ran off one boat day," said Mr. Carpenter. "And we've not seen either since. It must be 25 years. The neighbors took a whiparound for her and raised $28, and she stole $19 from old Lester's tea caddy."

"She did not," said Mrs. Carpenter. "I was at his place not five years ago, and he'd just been cleaning his kitchen table. He found her IOU for that $19. She never stole it at all."

THE Lady Lucinda comes to Madronna Island once a week. She is a fat little ship with a wicked roll to her, so that her passengers have often been seasick as she works her way from port to port—the Lucy calls at seven other islands before she sidles up to Madronna. But the mountains of Madronna give her a lee about 20 minutes before she actually comes alongside the government wharf, and that is enough time for the incapacitated to wash their wan faces and put their feet under them.

The whole island meets the Lucy. She is our only regular connection with the mainland. She brings the mail and the groceries and other necessities. Tonight she is bringing a new sow for Mr. Cuthbert.

The islanders are in the Carpenters' store, collecting their own groceries and making out their own bills. If a stranger comes in from a small boat wanting, say, nails, one of them will holler over the post office partition to ask Mr. Carpenter the price of five-inch nails the pound, and weigh them out for the stranger and make change from the old till which everybody can run. Jarge Gallagher, who keeps a home for retired machinery over on the channel side, will arrive late and be still collecting his groceries after everybody else has left. Jarge cannot read or write and the entire island knows it but only Mr. and Mrs. Carpenter *officially* know it, so they are the only ones who make out his store bills.

Mr. Carpenter cannot do it immediately because he is being the postmaster. Mrs. Carpenter cannot do it until after the island has finished having coffee and walnut slice and gossip in her kitchen.

The Lucy is showing only her riding lights as she edges toward the lanterns on the wharf. And then the darkness is split as the searchlight flashes on from the ship's bridge, and Irwin Hoffstater is catching the stern rope and tying her up and running like mad to catch the bow rope. It is Irwin's job to catch the ropes, for which he is paid two dollars a week. Blatant exploitation; but when they tried paying him ten he saved it up for three months and went to town and was knocked on the head and rolled before he was even out of the dock area. Irwin is a little simple and lives in a shack in the Carpenters' back yard where they can look out for him. After the rolling Captain McTague of the Lucy and Mr. Carpenter decided two dollars would be safer and the rest in kind.

But Irwin isn't so simple he doesn't know a scoop when he sees one. He came roaring through the store and into the Carpenters' kitchen. "Mr. Cuthbert," he bellowed, "Mr. Cuthbert! Your sow's having pigs on the Lucy's stern."

Mrs. Gathercole, the teacher, took that instant action which is convincing half the island that she is an excellent teacher. "Children," she said, gathering her class about her, "this will be an excellent opportunity for a biology lesson. We will go down and observe."

"Don't be indecent," snapped Elinor Filibruster, who is the island's most unpopular citizen.

"Nonsense, Elinor," said Mrs. Carpenter, swiftly switching the ideas on decency which she had herself been about to express. "How else are the children to learn?"

"I think it was the seasickness started her dropping them," said Captain McTague apologetically, puffing up behind Irwin.

There were 13 piglets. Mr. Cuthbert has given the runt to the school to raise. The children have called it Elinor after Elinor Filibruster, who went home mad.

W HAT do you do for a living on Madronna Island? People keep asking.

The Carpenters were not being greedy when they took over the official jobs. They came, years ago, to open the only store on the island. There are not enough islanders—56 or 57 depending on whether Captain O'Grady is in jail on the mainland—to support a store, so Mr. Carpenter also became the government road foreman. They have the post office because they are the only ones who would not tell all the others who gets welfare or is old enough to collect the old-age pension. And Mr. Carpenter doesn't make a cent out of being justice of the peace.

Everybody else on Madronna is an entrepreneur. Elwy Danson runs a gypo logging outfit. Thorn Robertson has a sawmill. Some are commercial fishermen. Some live off the land and sea, and get the cash they need by doing chores for retired pensioners. Some cut greenery for the wholesale florists. Captain O'Grady steals, which is when we need a justice of the peace.

Take the night Sam Hornick turned up at the Community Club to report that the plywood panelling had been stolen from the cottage he's building weekends. It was not the first theft Sam had suffered. In a fist he flourished the identification of the thief—a screwdriver, well known to all of us, bearing the Captain's initials (he stole the whole toolkit because it *did* have his initials).

"And this time," said Sam Hornick, "I'm not settling out of court."

Court was convened immediately. It is only on Madronna that a justice of the peace convenes court. This is because all Mr. Carpenter's cases are settled out of court.

"Captain, you're for it this time," he said. "It was a damnfool thing to use tools anybody could identify. If Mr. Hornick lays charges..."

"And I'm going to," said Sam Hornick.

"... you'll be off to prison for six months. You might as well admit it. Where's that panelling?"

"Over at Smugglers's Cove," said the ancient little Captain. He never fights the inevitable.

"All right. Now, Mr. Hornick. If you insist on taking the Captain in, I'll go along. But it would be wasteful. You'd get the panelling, but you'd have to spend another week-end putting it back in place..."

"Be worth it," said Sam Hornick, "just to know he's behind bars."

"...whereas, if you let me sentence him here and now—unofficial-like—to putting that panelling back on your walls..."

"I'd rather see him in a cell."

"...you would, of course, be entitled to damages. I believe you plan to finish the cottage in clapboard siding?"

"Y-e-s-s-s-s?" said Sam.

"Then I would further sentence the Captain—unofficial-like—to putting that siding in place and applying at least two coats of iron oil."

"That would take a month!" exploded the Captain.

"The other would take six. Well, Mr. Hornick?"

"I was planning on painting the cottage," said Sam Hornick. "White, with red trim."

"Then the sentence is altered to one coat of white undercoat and two of outside white, plus red trim."

The Captain is a graceful loser. "No hard feelings, Sam," he said. "I know just where I can pick up the siding you'll be needing. There's a stack of it, kiln-dried, over at Cooper..."

He had to be put under house arrest, with Mrs. Carpenter as warden.

ONE of the jobs always available on Madronna Island is picking greenery for the mainland florists. Until you get used to it and your muscles are in trim, picking greenery is back-breaking work. After that—if you like green wilderness—it is like being paid to play.

Greenery is used by florists for the background of their flower arrangements and for funeral wreaths, and it has to be durable. The chief source of it is salal, an evergreen bush with broad, tough, shiny leaves. There are also, at certain times of the year, swordfern, Oregon grape, arbutus boughs with their Japanese-garden shapes and their brilliant clusters of red berries, and moss. The moss we figured out for ourselves, and we now have one customer who uses a lot of it for making miniature drawing room gardens.

Most pickers are not reliable. They do it when the urge hits them or when they need a new engine for the boat or when the grates in the kitchen wood stove have given out for positively the last time and a new stove is required. So that if you prove you are reliable, month in and month out, you can demand and get a slightly better price.

But you have to meet the trade's needs. They don't want spoiled leaves on a branch. They like the sprays to lie flat. This means that the best picking is on the northern side of a mountain, where there is little sun to draw the leaves out of alignment.

Your equipment is a hatchet, slung in a holster from your belt, and a pair of pruning shears. The hatchet is for blazing your trail so that you won't get lost.

It is easy to get lost. Twenty feet from a trail you can be in forest so deep and untouched, so littered with deadfalls, so obliterating of even the sky, that you can almost believe that no human ever passed that way before; and maybe none has.

You mark out an area some 20 feet wide, and move back and forth across it, cropping as you go. This means that you are clambering over or under deadfalls, circling rocks, tripping on roots, being snagged by blackberry vines.

When the sack on your back is full—I forgot that piece of equipment, it has a heavy wire strung through the mouth to keep it agape—you cache your greenery and blaze the cache. At the end of the day, returning from the topmost point you have reached, you collect your caches—it takes several trips—and bring them down to the trail, where one of the other two regular pickers will collect them in a truck.

In the first month I got lost three times. The first two times, Lettie Danson and Marie Leclair, the other regular pickers, were able to rescue me. The third time was more embarrassing. I got stranded on a mountain ledge and couldn't go forward or back, up or down.

When they finally found me, they had to go for Irwin Hoffstater. Irwin is a little simple about some things, not safe from predators if he has much cash, so they pay him mostly in kind for his job of tying up the weekly boat. The latest piece of kind had been the stern rope from the SS Lady Lucinda—a little too old for her now, but fine for rescuing greenhorns.

Irwin anchored the rope to a cedar by a logging trail above, walked down the sheer mountainside holding to the rope, tied it firmly under my arms, walked back up the mountainside holding the rope, and pulled me up by the rope.

That, I can tell you, is a rope for which I have real feeling. Its next performance will be on Easter Monday, when Madronna takes on Cooper Island at tug-o'-war.

THE women of the Madronna Island Community Club sometimes sit in separate conclave. This is usually when they feel the men will be opposed to direct action.

They met on Wednesday to consider the case of Martin Voorhass, 12. Martin lives on a fishboat with his father, who abuses him. The abuse has been reported from different islands to the police, but Mr. Voorhass must have second sight because by the time Sergeant Munro gets to where the offence was committed Mr. Voorhass and his boat have gone somewhere else. Tracing it seemed impossible until Wednesday when old Mildred Stonehenge phoned Mrs. Carpenter to get the women together because she had spotted the boat in Beachcombers' Bay. Mildred has been 91 years on Madronna, and she knows a boat even when it has had its rigging adjusted and been renamed and repainted.

The women convened at 2 p.m., Mrs. Carpenter in the chair, Elinor Filibruster secretary.

"The Voorhass boat came into the bay mid-morning," reported Mildred. "I had the glasses on it. The man ate at a table in the cuddy, herring and bread, I think, with a knife and fork. Every once in a while he would throw a piece of bread to the boy on the deck and the boy ate it with his fingers. After a while the man went out on the deck and threw the boy overboard. He kept dunking him with a boat hook. That water isn't above 30 degrees Fahrenheit. I got a bead on him with my rifle but I was afraid if I dropped him the boy might drown. He was pretty well gone before the man fished him out with the boathook and tossed him down on the deck. I move the Madronna Island Community Club kidnap Martin Voorhass."

"That would be illegal," said Elinor Filibruster,

nevertheless noting the motion in the minutes book.

"Second the motion," said Lettie Danson.

"All in favor? Carried," said Mrs. Carpenter.

"The boat's tied up now," said Mildred. "The boy was in the cuddy, last I looked, and the man's on the wharf sharpening a saw. I move we name a committee of Lettie Danson and Marie Leclair to kidnap the boy. I'll ride shotgun."

"All in favor? Carried," said Mrs. Carpenter.

The meeting adjourned to the bluff above Beachcombers' Bay. "Just march straight past the man onto the boat and grab the boy between you," said Mildred, "and then march straight off. If the man makes a move, I'll handle him."

Half an hour later we were back at the Community Hall with Martin Voorhass. We had been joined by three terrified males, Mr. Carpenter, Elwy Danson and Doc Filbert, who is retired on the island and gets $500 a year from the government for looking after emergencies. The men were terrified because the island women had not only broken the law, they had conspired to break the law and it was down in the minutes book. Mr. Carpenter tried to throw the book in the stove but Mrs. Carpenter sat on it. "It's our minutes," she said. "Look at that boy."

He was black and blue over almost every inch of his body, had a broken nose and three broken fingers. He's going to live with the Dansons until we figure it out, which will probably be until he is old enough to be a partner in Elwy's logging outfit.

"But why," moaned Mr. Carpenter at Mildred, "did you have to shoot?"

"Does it matter?" she asked. "He lit out so fast he must be half way to hell. He won't stop to tell a cop. He was going to jump the girls and I had to stop him. I just pinked him in the left cheek of his bum."

WHAT makes cutting greenery for the mainland florists a good job, if you like the wilds, is that it puts you right into them, almost makes you part of them.

It is hard work; but you can never tell when you will come across a doe nursing her fawn, or a young buck rubbing the velvet from his proud new horns, or—once—two bucks having it out in a bit of a forest clearing while a doe stood smugly by.

I got up in a tree and watched the whole thing; and if you ask me, there was a lot of put-on about that fight. You could have set those bucks to ballet music. It was the oldest one that got the girl, at least I think so; he had the most horns. But I didn't see any blood on anybody.

Not that I would wish to give the impression that the nature I find on Madronna sets man an example of gentleness and conducts even its battles in a purely stylized fashion. Not much.

The eagle I surprised on a bough eight feet from the ground munching a 10-pound salmon had manslaughter in mind. Of me. Because he was startled into dropping the tail half of his salmon at my feet. Only the trees were so close together that he got his huge wings all tangled up in them and that just made him madder, and he squeaked. Yes; I am sorry to have to report it. But that was the sound this noblest of birds made when he was mad. He squeaked.

He went on flopping around and squeaking until I got out of there—a record for cross-forest sprinting, I should think—and he took his salmon back.

He had his reasons, of course, which would have mitigated sentence. But the gulls we saw trying to drown a deer were just bent on murder for fun.

There were four of us down on the shore, collecting drift.

Old Mildred Stonehenge doesn't cut greenery any more, but she likes to collect drift, although only the drift the sea has shaped into animals or birds. She has a drift zoo around her place up on the bluff which she intends to leave as a park to the Madronna Island Community Club when she dies. That will not be for some time. Mildred is only 91 and means to beat the island record, which is 106.

Anyway, there we were on the shore. A deer was swimming from Madronna Point across Head Bay and was just about half-way to Head Point when a flock of gulls started to dive-bomb him. They were extraordinarily organized about it, coming down in squadron formation, one after the other, and hitting him on the head and pushing his nose under water.

He was pretty well a goner, stopped still in the water and floundering and bleeding, when Mildred got her gun. She never travels without her gun. She picked off three of the gulls, one, two, three; and that was that. Demoralized the rest of the squadron, and the deer got under way again and the last we saw he was stumbling ashore at Head Point, looking beat.

Now why in the world would a bunch of gulls want to murder a deer?

Maybe it was target practice. Because they do the same thing when they find a herring ball. This is very foolish of the herring, and you would think they would learn. But at certain times they are so overcome by a desire for togetherness that they get themselves all packed into a great big ball; and a gull always sees them.

This gull summons the tribe—I will say that for gulls, they share—and they hit that herring ball one after the other, each nipping off a herring and keeping the ball rolling forward so that the herring can't disconnect.

Mildred never picks off a gull that is herring fishing. She hunts for the pot herself.

THE matter of resurrection has been under discussion at the Davises. Ken and Flo Davis adopted Ronnie and Penny Falkner when the rest of their family were killed in an auto accident. Ronnie is nine and Penny, who is a little retarded, is five. Penny has settled in just fine, but Ronnie wants to be convinced that sometime, somewhere, their whole family will be together again. He is doing his best to be a good son to the Davises in the meantime.

That was what sent him rushing for the flyswatter when the hornet got in. It was a very big hornet, shiny black and elegantly patterned in yellow. Rather sluggish; it was late in the fall. Ronnie would have swatted it but Charlie Jo stayed his hand.

"Would you kill a queen and her people?" he asked.

Charlie Jo is Indian, 18, leads the island rock band, wears the most expensive, latest-style work boots on Madronna, and holds that man is not the superior product of nature, just one of many. "That's a queen hornet," he told Ronnie. "She's got her people inside her. She will find a quiet place for the winter and next spring she will lay her eggs and there will be new hornets."

So the children got her some honey, which she waded in but didn't seem to eat, and they had to wash her by floating her in the wash basin. It chipped a little off one of her wings. They called her Pinkie.

Unfortunately, the next day Pinkie was joined by about 20 other large, elegant hornets, and the next day by about 100, and the third day there were 200 of them droning slowly around—the count may not have been exact. How they got in nobody could find out. As the light faded they would cluster around the tops of the windows, lying with their heads together, sometimes stroking each other with their feelers. There were a few very small hornets, but they all seemed to end up dead on the floor.

The Davises are easygoing people and the hornets did not attack so the humans and the hornets coexisted. For visitors who were afraid to coexist, the Davises hung mosquito nets from the ceiling. Of course the entire island came to see the hornets; the entire island always does attend upon any phenomenon. Even Elinor Filibruster, who is the most objectionable person on Madronna, came and sat under a mosquito net and said it was a disgrace to have vermin flying around like that and kept uttering little screams and was stung by Pinkie.

At least Charlie Jo and Ronnie and Penny and Ken and Flo Davis say she was stung by Pinkie. Doc Filbert, who is retired on Madronna, says she just swelled up with hysteria. The rest of the island, none of whom had been stung by the Davises' hornets, held that Pinkie had shown remarkably good taste.

At about this time the hornets began to vanish as mysteriously as they had arrived. "Going off to sleep for the winter," Charlie Jo said. And after a while they were down to about 10, Pinkie still one of them, you could tell by the chipped wing. And then one morning Ronnie found Pinkie dead on the floor.

He cried horribly, like a grown man who can't stop himself, until the Davises got Charlie Jo. Charlie sat with his arm around Ronnie until the sobs stopped.

"You must take Pinkie in your hand now," he said, "and carry her out to the maple on the point. We will cover her with maple leaves, and in the spring she will lay the eggs of her people in the place where hornets go when they are done with here."

"But how can you know?" cried Ronnie. "How can you know?"

"For that," said Charlie Jo, "you have to believe."

ONE of the more unlikely partnerships on Madronna is that of Mrs. Carpenter, who is Good, and that of Richard James, who is Bad. Richard James is a freelance writer who has been living on a houseboat in June Harbor for the last couple of years. He is Bad—in Mrs. Carpenter's view, that is—because he has had three commonlaw wives in a row.

It is spring on Madronna now, and the present co-operation involves the Cuthbert's manure pile. Mrs. Carpenter has written three times to the Department of Health about that manure pile, which is ancient, large and smelly, and has had only form letters in reply. Richard took more direct action.

"Of course it's a mess," he said thoughtfully the other evening as we were sitting in the Carpenters' kitchen, "but it could be useful in every garden on the island. I think we'll have to enlist Captain O'Grady. How much, Jim," he asked Mr. Carpenter, "do you think the Cap could get from the islanders for a trailer-load of well-rotted manure? That small trailer of Irwin's?"

"About five dollars, I'd say," said Mr. Carpenter.

"If you think you're going to get the captain into an honest line of work, you don't know the captain," said Mrs. Carpenter tartly.

"Honest!" exclaimed Richard, shocked. "Certainly not. I was thinking of the captain *stealing* the manure. It would be simple. He would just have to back Irwin's trailer up to the rear end of the pile, out of sight of the Cuthberts' house and barn, and fill it up."

31

"You cannot get good from evil," said Mrs. Carpenter severely.

"No," agreed Richard, "but you can get asparagus."

Without any overt co-operation the team got the supply line working. Mrs. Carpenter, entirely honestly and above-board, asked Mr. Cuthbert what he would charge her if she sent Irwin up to his manure pile for a couple of loads of manure. Irwin is a kind of simple-minded dependent of the Carpenters. Mr. Cuthbert said 50 cents a load, since Irwin would be doing the work. Irwin collected two loads —from the back of the pile—and Mrs. Carpenter paid Mr. Cuthbert a dollar.

That opened both the manure pile and the money question, and all Richard had to do was drop a couple of words—"five dollars"—in the captain's ear. After that the Cuthberts' manure pile began to be seriously depleted and all the island gardens to be fertilized. Irwin was happy to oblige the captain with the loan of his trailer.

This suggestion of a new business enterprise served to heal a breach which had opened between Richard and the captain. Richard had visited the captain's still in the mine shaft in the mountain, and been distressed by the captain's method of operating.

"You are being too greedy." he announced sternly. "In the distilling process, the harmful esters which increase such problems as hangovers come off during the first and last third of the operation. After this you must retain only the middle third."

The captain would infinitely have preferred two-thirds less work, but Richard was ruthless. He simply poured away the offending two-thirds.

"But I believe," he told us that night, "that we will have to let him raise his price per gallon from $4 to $8. Otherwise he might be discouraged into non-production."

There are some of us islanders who, with the captain, would be content with $4 gin and more hangovers, but in face of the stern partnership of morality and immorality represented by Mrs. Carpenter and Richard we are impotent.

AN isolated island like Madronna produces distinctive people. Perhaps this is true of all small communities.

The people are not lined up in streets, to be disciplined into conformity by their neighbors, the staff at the office, the zoning bylaws. They are free, as it is not possible to be free in a city. Yet, on the other hand, they are bound as a city does not bind them.

They are bound to stand on their own feet. They are also bound, when trouble comes, to help their neighbors and accept help from their neighbors. There are few institutions to move in and do it for them. In a city, if they didn't like the family down the block, they would simply deal them out of their lives. On Madronna, if they drive their truck over the cliff, it may be the disliked family that hitches the block and tackle to pull them back.

The result is that they expand. They don't change basically; but they begin to look and act more like themselves.

Take Tom and Helen Jessup. When they arrived here they were a pleasant, nondescript couple. They haven't, Madronna thinks, much money; Tom is retired as a not-very-successful accountant from a small prairie town. They bought one of the less desirable of Mr. Carpenter's lots at June Harbor, behind the waterfront, and put up a tiny house. They have no running water and no power plant; but that tiny house is one of the happiest places on Madronna to visit.

It is full of small household gods—like the two bread-and-butter plates left over from the dinner set they were given when they married, and now hung on the wall behind the kitchen table. Each of their possessions reminds them of some past joy or sorrow, and it is always kept in its

33

exactly right place. When their grandchildren arrive, or the island children, and one of the household gods ends up in pieces on the floor, that is its exactly right place, too. No thing is ever allowed to take precedence over a person or, for that matter, an animal. They comfort the destroyer while they pick up the pieces.

I daresay that is why they are down to two bread-and-butter plates from the wedding dinner set.

They work endlessly in their garden, which is one of the island's showplaces. But they do not hate any of the creatures that contest with them for its produce. They lost their first plantings of peas and corn and beans to the crows. They fixed it by covering future plantings with fine wire mesh and enjoying the crows.

The crows are intelligent and humorous. They take a good deal of malicious pleasure out of driving Biff, the Jessups' dog, out of his mind with rage by stealing the bread which Tom and Helen have put out for them to steal.

Tom and Helen are even more delighted with the squirrels that steal their tulip blossoms, and, indeed, the squirrels are most entertaining to watch. They nip off a bud just below the bloom and sit there pealing the petals carefully back, like the skin of a banana, eat the yellow heart, and toss the rest away. After which Tom or Helen slips out and picks up the abandoned bud and puts it in the birdbath, where it blooms.

They not only enjoy the tulip but the squirrel—and still have the tulip. It is a conservation of enjoyment which certain islanders we could all mention would never understand.

On another occasion we may mention Dan Potter. Dan Potter is reported to have been mean in 19 different places on the mainland, which was why he moved so often. He kept wearing the neighbors out. But on Madronna he has achieved absolutely classical meanness.

OF all the islanders only Lester Cholmondeley and old Robbie Robinson made the mistake of building in sight of each other. This happened because Lester sold Robbie a chunk of his acreage and they were under the impression they were friends. The impression departed when Robbie built a neat cottage (Lester's shack is what Mrs. Carpenter describes as a proper pigsty), and the two proved to have totally different life styles.

Or, as Lester describes it: "The man's a madman. Hangs his washing out every Monday morning, and scrubs his kitchen floor twice a week. As for his strawberries, they're the worst fiddling things you ever saw. Down on his knees he is to them, half the day. And carrying bowls of them to the ladies, and them sitting him down for a cup of coffee and a cinnamon bun. And he's hardly ever out of the things. Right now he's got an early strain going, under those storm windows by his south wall."

Robbie's attitude to the relationship was less complex. As a clean, decent, hard-working citizen, he simply looked DOWN on Lester.

We were sitting in the Carpenter kitchen the other evening when the latest round of hostilities got under way. There was a bang on the back door and a very tall, very clean, very angry old man came in. Robbie. He had come to demand that Mr. Carpenter, as the island's justice of the peace, call the police and have charges laid against Lester for stealing his very first strawberry crop of the year.

Mrs. Carpenter at once cut him a piece of the hot spice cake she'd thrown together when the children and I came in, and poured him a cup of coffee. But while he would have the cake and the coffee, he would not have peace. He did not leave, stamping his feet, until Mr. Carpenter had promised to come down in the morning and view the evidence.

Mr. Carpenter was very concerned. He does not believe that man should sit in judgment on man and always tries to ensure that cases arising on Madronna are settled out of court.

"They're a real problem, those two," he said. "Getting worse and worse. Whenever there's a dinner at the community hall I have to borrow a kid from the school to sit between them in the truck when I drive them over. They won't even scrape their skinny shanks. I don't suppose you'd have old Lester under house arrest?" he asked Mrs. Carpenter hopefully.

"Not unless he has a bath first," said Mrs. Carpenter, and the justice of the peace sighed.

He was still sighing when the second angry justice-seeker arrived. Old Lester brought some rhubarb for the Carpenters, and insisted on laying charges against old Robbie for stealing his banties. "There's two of my best birds racked up in his kitchen right now," he said wrathfully, "all ready for tomorrow's lunch."

Mr. Carpenter was finally forced to promise that he would go down on the morrow and inspect the evidence.

He kept his word.

At noon he appeared at old Robbie's place where he found, indeed, that two plum bantie hens had just been grilled to perfection. He helped old Robbie eat them. After that he went along to old Lester's where he found, indeed, a bowl of ripe red strawberries. He helped old Lester eat them. After that he told each of them, separately, that they wouldn't be able to prosecute this time.

No evidence.

36

OLD Robbie keeps his fishing boat tied up at the government float, which he is not supposed to do. The government float is supposed to be kept free for transient vessels, and old Robbie is not a transient.

Police Sergeant Munro has tried to make the principle clear to him, and so have other islanders with boats, who like to tie up there to get their mail and groceries and can't, because old Robbie already is tied up.

Old Robbie has never bothered to reply to the complaints, even the sergeant's. He just looks at the complainer, managing to present a picture of silent, unmoved stubbornness, until the complainer's tongue runs down, and then goes on doing what he has always done.

In the case of the sergeant, because the sergeant, after all, is the law, he goes down and moves his boat temporarily, takes up a position just off the wharf and stays there until the sergeant has gone. Then he moves back to what he considers his rightful place, if necessary moving any other boat that has pre-empted it.

The situation has led to a non-settlement settlement which is typical of the islands. Old Robbie stays where he intends to stay. The other islanders tie up alongside his boat, instead of the float, using his boat as an extension of the float (although carefully; islanders can hate each other to pieces but they are united in their respect for boats).

The non-settlement has its advantages. If there is nothing else to talk about there is always the stubbornness of old Robbie.

The trouble is, he is stubborn about other things; practically everything, in fact.

He is 87, and last year the islanders decided he really ought not to go fishing. It would be all right if he went out for a few hours to catch the late afternoon tide, when there would be plenty of other boats about to keep an eye on him. But he has kept his commercial fishing licence and he likes to go out before daybreak and come back with a boatload of fish; and that is what he has kept on doing.

To be truthful, it isn't just old Robbie's safety we worry about, it's all those fish. Have you ever been presented with a wheelbarrow full of salmon, fresh from the ocean, which have to be canned at once if they are to preserve that fleeting flavor which no commercial canner ever does preserve? When you have guests coming for lunch and your stove is already covered with preserving kettles full of the crabs the children caught in the seaweed when the tide was out?

Every household of Madronna can count on at least three barrow loads of salmon from old Robbie every summer. Mrs. Carpenter is unlucky. Because she always feeds him cinnamon buns or cheesecake when he comes for his mail, he gives her five or six barrow loads.

One can't waste good food.

And none of us has the courage of the summer visitor, who once stood on her cottage porch and screamed at old Robbie, "You take those nasty smelly salmon back and put them in the ocean where you found them!"

It just meant, of course, that Mrs. Carpenter got an extra barrow load of salmon that year.

W HEN Lennie Danson, 11, was not home for supper at 6:30, three hours after school had closed, his mother put out the "trouble-come-all" message on the party line, and everybody on the island that could be reached went at once to the Dansons'.

The difficulty was that Lennie could have run into trouble on the mountains, by the sea, in the marshes—anywhere in a fairly large island of mainly wilderness. Jim Carpenter, the justice of the peace, was organizing search parties when Charlie Jo, who is 18, arrived. "I think," said Charlie, getting Mr. Carpenter's eye, "that we better send out the kids first. They'll know where he might have gone. Down to his cod line (most of the kids keep live lines where they think the fishing is best, secret from the adults, of course) or to some of the caves or to his fort."

"They've been forbidden to dig forts," said Mary Gathercole, the teacher.

"That's what I mean," said Charlie Jo.

So Mr. Carpenter gave Charlie the go sign and he went out to the 12 school children who were gathered, subdued, in the garden. He split them into teams of two. "Make your own arrangements, fast," he told them. "Go where you think Lennie might have gone. If he's in trouble or you can't find him, come straight back here."

Waiting like that is as hard a job as you'll have in your lifetime. It was more than an hour and getting dark before Martin, the Dansons' foster son, came running back to tell us that Lennie was trapped in his fort. "A rock kind of settled on his foot as he was coming out. He's lying on his face. Bob stayed with him."

Mrs. Danson called Sergeant Munro on Cooper Island

and asked him to send miners and the ambulance boat. We went to the fort. It was a hole dug by Lennie and his friends under the edge of a huge sandstone rock. As he had been crawling out the rock had settled and seized and crushed his left foot.

Doc Filbert, who is retired on Madronna, gave Lennie a shot to knock him out. Captain O'Grady took charge. He is the island's thief, but in one of his former careers he was a miner. First he had the men carry a big flat granite rock and place it under the lip of the sandstone rock—"in case she settles some more." Then he crawled into the fort on one side of Lennie and sent Charlie Jo in on the other. Charlie is tall, like a man, but still with the slightness of 18. They pawed the gravel from under Lennie's left foot—it was wet with blood—out to Elwy Danson and Mr. Carpenter, lying flat behind them, who pawed it on to others.

Three minutes after they started the sandstone rock lurched and was halted by the granite rock.

No words. No movements except for the pawing men. Hardly even a breath.

"All right," said Captain O'Grady, after forever, "take him." And the two men who had been waiting drew Lennie Danson slowly, carefully, the broken foot supported by the thieving little captain and his young Indian helper, out of the tomb.

Elwy Danson and Mr. Carpenter yanked the two rescuers out of there a lot quicker than that. And as Mr. Carpenter held Charlie Jo close in his arms, the great sandstone rock cracked on the granite rock and flattened the fort. A good fort it had been, too, cunningly set to defend the mountain pass.

"Kid country," said Charlie Jo, to deny the terror that his trembling spoke, "I used to live there myself."

IT was Richard James, our freelance writer, who some years ago suggested a means of improving the pinched Madronna economy. Summer visitors. "Don't be humble about the accommodation you have to offer," he said. "Boast about it. But don't try it on ordinary people like plumbers or lawyers or grocers. They'd have too much sense. Aim for the academics."

Most of the accommodation, it is true, is a little wanting. For instance, my house has six bedrooms, but to get to three of them you have to walk through the other three. If you are in an outside upstairs bedroom and want to go to the bathroom, you have to walk through the inner bedroom, down the stairs, and through the downstairs inner and outer bedrooms to the bathroom. After we started getting visitors the Carpenters, who run the store, had to lay in an extra stock of chamber pots.

Mrs. Carpenter, who is a long-time resident, says island houses are this way because island men would always rather build around a rock or a treestump than take it out.

Our ads, written by Mr. Carpenter who sounds exactly like the good, honest old rural days (because he never left them, I guess), have attracted a steady stream of academics, and one fireman. This year Mr. Carpenter is including the Cuthberts' loft, which has been demiced by three cats and a terrier, and the upstairs of the lighthouse. If there is a law that says you can't rent parts of a lighthouse, kindly do not draw it to our attention. Dan Masterson, the lighthouse keeper, wants the money to buy a bred Percheron mare. He says that in a couple of years there won't be gasoline for trucks, and the demand for draft horses ought to be big.

Our changeover day for visitors, Richard suggested,

should be Sunday, because the once-a-week ship from the mainland calls on Saturday. This means that visitors have to get off the ship at Cooper Island and travel by Noel Sorenson's small boat to Madronna ($1 for adults, 50 cents for children). It pleases our academics by convincing them that they are really going to the back of the beyond, and is also good for the island economy.

Noel dumps all his passengers at the government wharf, although he could just as easily take them to our separate floats. But that would mean that they would not have to use Irwin Hoffstater's taxi ($1 for adults, 50 cents for children). Irwin's taxi is very popular with visiting children. In what city could you find a taxi that spits flames through its front floor boards and has to be pushed to the crest of every mountain?

At first we thought we would have to give up picking greenery for the mainland florists—one of our few cash crops—to look after our guests. Not at all. They love to get back to nature and pick too, giving us the pickings. The anthropologists, who are used to getting out and about rough terrain, have turned out to be the best pickers, so we rather favor anthropologists.

They also go out with the children to catch crabs in the seaweed, search for oysters on the beach, dig clams, jig for herring and tear their clothes to pieces picking black-berries. An academic who has spent most of the day finding his own food and has been topped up with Captain O'Grady's bootleg gin goes to bed early and happy, and pays the most exorbitant prices for room and board.

This country ought to hire Richard James to sort out its economic problems. He lives in a houseboat to avoid real estate taxes.

MILDRED Stonehenge will be 92 on May 5 and the 57 inhabitants of Madronna Island (56 if Captain O'Grady is in jail on the mainland) will celebrate her birthday with a dinner-concert-dance at the community hall (infants sleeping on the stage).

Mildred's biography is already being written up by Johnny Cuthbert for the Madronna newspaper which is edited by our freelance writer, Richard James. At the moment the newspaper is written with chalk on two of the school's blackboards, and the whole island goes in once a week to read it, not necessarily at the same time but when it is convenient for them to do so—when it is frequently not convenient for Mrs. Gathercole, the teacher.

The children are the reporters and it was Johnny who was sent along to interview Mildred—taking me as bodyguard because he and Mildred had recently had a difference over a slingshot and a window. Mildred was gracious, though. She greeted us both with mugs of hot blackberry wine, and prepared to look back.

She was born on Madronna. She could remember hoeing rows of cabbages a quarter mile long when her father raised vegetables to sell on the mainland. She could remember hiding from the hoeing in the underwater cave at June Harbor. "You know about that?" she asked Johnny sharply. "Yeah," said Johnny. "Well, don't go blabbing it to the grownups," said Mildred, giving me an intimidating look.

She had been married at 18 and raised six children. She was mournfully proud that she had survived all but two of them and sorry her husband wasn't still around. He'd been killed in a logging accident. He was milking a cow in the barn while she and her eldest son were cutting a large

43

maple tree alongside it. "Meant to drop it by the barn," she said, "and dropped it *on* the barn." She looked regretfully down the years.

"Killed the cow, too," she said.

Charlie Jo, who is 18 and the leader of the Madronna rock band, is in charge of the concert in Mildred's honor. They are dropping rock for the evening and presenting folk. Charlie has spent many hours with Mildred at the piano in the community hall trying to recapture her special song. Charlie can't read music (and in any case there is no music to be read) but he has a very accurate ear. Mildred has been humming her song and he has been picking it out note by note on the piano. Mildred thinks he's got it just about right. But the trouble is, she can't remember the lyrics.

"I think," she says, "it was called Two Little Girls in Blue. And there was a line in it about 'You can't holler down our rain barrel,' and one about 'You can't something our cellar door.' And it might have ended, 'But we have drifted apart.' Or that was maybe another song. But it was a great song. Maisie Hooper and I sang it at the school concert, and we wore blue sunbonnets that my mother made, and blue pinnies."

Charlie has talked to all the oldtimers on the island, and some of them can kind of remember a song like that, especially the rain barrel; but not enough for the school children to sing it for Mildred while the rock band plays it. The school children will just have to hum. It makes Charlie rather sad.

"On her birthday," he says, "a woman ought to be able to have her own music."

WE adopted Coonie shortly after we moved into our house on Madronna Island. Coonie is a wild raccoon with only three legs (left hind being missing). We had been warned not to make pets of raccoons because they never stop being wild and may well take the end of a finger along with the offered bread. But who could be harsh to a three-legged coon?

Coonie, anyway, had obviously had relations with former occupants of the house, because the first time he came to call he simply gave a peremptory bang to the kitchen window which opens inward, pushed it open, stepped to the kitchen counter and opened the bread box. We were enchanted, if wary, and all the more so when he took his slice of bread, climbed to the top of the old leather kitchen rocking chair, and sat there eating and rocking.

He will even let some people sit in the rocker while he is using the back of it. Our family is acceptable, and Charlie Jo and Irwin Hoffstater and some others. But Mr. Carpenter, the storekeeper, is too tall. He gets in Coonie's view of the room, so Coonie nips him out of there pronto. These are friendly nips, however, no blood drawn. A visiting district foreman lost a chunk of his scalp when he used Coonie's chair without permission.

On the whole our relations with Coonie are cordial but respectful. It was with his relatives and friends that the trouble arose. His mate arrived first. She climbed the drainpipe alongside the kitchen window—we catch rainwater on the house's various roofs—and banged for Coonie's attention. He went to the breadbox, fetched a slice, handed it out to her, and shut the window on her.

The next night there were two more raccoons demanding handouts, and by the end of a month there were 27 of them, eating 10 loaves of Mr. Carpenter's sliced bread every night. It wasn't only, at the time, that we couldn't afford that much bread; it was that they had got downright intimidating about the whole thing.

The raccoons came as soon as the sun was down. If we did not immediately deliver the bread, they banged on the glass doors that open on the front porch. They climbed the various drain pipes and banged on windows, they sat on the various roofs and banged. When there are bandit faces lined up at the French doors, bandit faces at almost every window, banging from every direction, and a continuous caterwauling going on, it is possible to feel besieged.

Not to put too fine a point on it, we were cowering in the kitchen one night when Charlie Jo arrived. He was furious. "Why do you let them get away with it?" he demanded.

He went storming out with his flashlight. "Scram! Beat it!" we could hear him bellowing. "Git man. You heard me! Come down off that roof! Move man! I said move!" One by one the bandit faces disappeared, the banging stopped, the caterwauling faded. "And don't come back!" hollered Charlie Jo. And then his voice gentled. "All right, you can stay," he said to somebody.

Coming back in he spoke to Coonie, who was still rocking placidly. "You can give your wife some bread," he said, "but she stays outside. Understand?"

Coonie got his wife a slice of bread.

We would have liked to think it was because he is Indian and young, a sort of modern Hiawatha, that his furry friends understood Charlie Jo. But it wasn't. They just recognized the voice of authority.

Or, as Charlie put it, "They're not stupid. They just think you're stupid."

WE have this visiting peacock.

The Cuthberts, who farm on the plateau behind us, bought him and four peahens when they decided they could make a good thing out of peacocks. Captain O'Grady brought them on his boat and put in at our bay instead of the Madronna Island government wharf. He stopped by for a cup of coffee. When we got to his boat for a look at the new fowl, the hens were still there but the peacock was gone.

We fanned out for a thorough search, because peacocks cost money. Also, the raccoons might get him, or the mink. Not a sign. Finally I retreated to the house to make fresh coffee for the searchers. There, with his gorgeous tail at peak elevation, slowly turning before the three-way mirror in the kitchen, was the missing bird. I rang the bell on the porch and everybody came to admire the peacock admiring himself. He was removed to the Cuthberts' new peacock run which is surrounded by an eight-foot wire fence, otherwise the coons and mink would have them.

Two hours later the peacock was back before the three-way mirror in the kitchen, tail up, turning slowly from side to side, admiring his whole beautiful self from every angle. He was taken back to the henrun. He returned to the mirrows. He was taken back to the henrun. He returned to the mirrors.

Among other oddities, our house is rather excessively supplied with mirrors. They were put in by the owners before, as Mr. Carpenter put it, "She went stir-crazy in our island fastness and made him take her back to the mainland."

Besides the three-way mirror in the kitchen there is a full-length mirror on every door, in every bedroom, on the

47

bathroom ceiling. The top of the big kitchen table was also covered by a mirror, but I had that removed at once because it wouldn't have lasted two days with the kids banging around and me putting down hot pots. Besides, it gave an unflattering view of double chins, receding chins and over-large noses. Why a devotee of mirrors would choose to be reflected from that angle is a puzzle. The island women decided the mirror should be lent to Elinor Filbruster, whom they all heartily dislike, but you can't be mean. Elinor loves to look at herself and the Filibruster income doesn't run to plate glass. (We are very generous with the property of off-island owners.)

I was awfully glad the mirror had gone to Elinor before the peacock found it. He found every other mirror in the house, even the one on the bathroom ceiling. The kids booby-trapped him once by filling the bath under it. His indignation was audible across the harbor. He became so involved with mirrors that the Cuthberts were afraid he would fail in his duty toward his flock. But he must have paused in passing. They're all sitting.

The Cuthberts have sent down his food. We have accepted that you can't keep a determined peacock out and named him Narcissus. Narce for short.

He never bothers to answer to his name. He is really an extremely stupid bird. Occasionally one of his fellow residents, unable to bear him any longer, will goose him in his elegant tailfeathers, producing some nasty remarks from Narce but moving him no further than the next mirror.

If you have peacocks, think it might be ornamental to have them preening around the house as well as the garden and are considering introducing them to mirrors, don't.

Peacocks don't housebreak.

GETTING the mainland goat is a perfectly acceptable island occupation. But the way it was being got that day was earning the strong disapprobation of our resident freelance writer, Richard James.

It was a sunny spring afternoon. Richard and I were taking the sun on a grassy bluff above Ching Narrows where the salmon, in their season, run. Standing out in the channel, but beginning to stray perilously close to the seaweeded shore, was one of those expensive sports boats with two fishing chairs bolted to its stern. The chairs were occupied by two fishermen who were enjoying bad luck.

At the very edge of the weeds two fishermen in an Indian one-lunger were pulling in fish as fast as they could put their lines out. They were Charlie Jo, who *is* Indian and usually the last word in island elegance, and Johnny Cuthbert, who is neither. They had pulled the hair over their faces and were slouching like slobs. Charlie, who is 18, looked about 14, and Johnny, who is 12, looked 10. Doubtless they were conversing in grunts. They were being the savages pulling in the salmon which those white men in the fancy boat couldn't even persuade to bite.

In fact, as we knew, they were pulling in rock cod, because this is not the salmon season.

"Charlie," Richard bellowed at last, "come up here!"

Hitching their boat with a rock on its painter, the boys obligingly did so.

"Why the hell," demanded Richard, "do you have to hold us up to shame? You're just trying to get that boat in the weeds. In fact, you have. Why not change the script to the Noble Red Man?"

Charlie considered, grinned, combed his hair, wiped his face with a handkerchief, said, "Certainly, sir," and handed the comb to Johnny. "You, Johnny," said Richard, "behave with reserve." "Huh?" said Johnny. "Hold your shoulders back and keep your mouth shut," said Richard.

From the back they both looked slim and proud as they took the one-lunger out to the mired sports craft. Charlie, who had thrown a tarp over most of their catch, presented a long silver fish to the fishermen ("must have caught a stray white spring," said Richard) and sent Johnny into the water under their boat to free its propeller of weeds. When Johnny had surfaced, they took their own boat in tow and piloted the sports craft back to safe waters. Then they waved their friends upon their way and came back to shore. We joined them.

"Charlie done real good," Johnny reported to Richard. "He give them the white spring salmon he caught. And he talked just like you."

At that moment the betraying clarity of air over water brought us the words of one of the departing fishermen: "Pleasant pair of young savages," he said.

Charlie Jo subdued his grin to a ghost and took the tarp off the rock cod.

"May I cut you some fillets?" he asked.

GOVERNMENT grants can be very useful. But it is not necessary to tell the government all. This year Charlie Jo, who is the head of our jobless teenagers, and Mr. Carpenter, who spoke for the Community Club, neglected to mention that they were recruiting some unorthodox labor.

The grant is to provide a dam to retain some of the rain which falls on Madronna Island during the winter months and now runs right off. This should keep wells from going dry in the summer, as they now do.

What Charlie and Mr. Carpenter neglected to tell the government was that the dam builders will be beavers. Charlie arranged with his mainland kinsmen for the delivery of three pair before the young were due to arrive and they are now busily engaged in the marshy upper reaches of Clare Creek.

Madronna has deemed the beaver to have floated in on log booms since it is against the law to move wild animals from a place where they are to a place where they are not. This is a defence which should stand up because a beaver did float in once and he set up housekeeping in the swamp above the Davises. The Davises had piped water from the swamp to their house, and the first thing the beaver did was cut off their intake pipe.

Ken Davis went up and cleared it. He suspected beaver because of the beaverlike chips lying about though he never saw the beaver, so he raised the level of the intake pipe. The beaver closed it every night all that spring and summer, and Ken opened it every morning. If Ken had found him there would probably have immediately been no beaver on Madronna. But a mink got him first and the road crew (Mr. Carpenter and whichever property owner is working off his taxes) found the body.

The point, though, is that in the summer when one beaver worked and successively raised the level of the Davises' swamp, no well below that swamp ran dry.

Clare Creek is a good holding place for the beavers, but their eventual duty on Madronna lies elsewhere.

The government-grant crew (four males, three females) will not just take the government money and do nothing. Below the top of one of our larger mountains is a spring-fed swamp in the midst of a natural cup big enough to hold a real lake. The workers will enlarge the present dribble to drain the swamp and let the water flow down the mountainside. They hope to manage the stream so it will drop from natural cup to natural cup (and the landowners below say they better or!). Then, while the big swampy cup at the top is virtually empty of water they will clear it of vegetation, so that the water will be clean. In the fall they will plug the big cup's outlet—that is the dam the government thinks they are building, but actually Elwy Danson will do it in a day with a bulldozer—and by next spring Madronna should have a lake.

The beavers will then be transferred from the Clare to the big lake and the little lakes below it, where for the next few years they will be in charge of building Madronna's water conservation system.

"Of course," said Charlie Jo, "eventually we'll have too many beavers. They don't like us using their water and they'll try to hog it. So then we'll transport the excess to Cooper Island." Cooper is a rich island with blacktop roads and a complete waterworks system. It will not want beavers.

"But they're a law-abiding bunch over there," said Charlie comfortably. "They'll make the wildlife people fly them somewhere else."

$\mathcal{S}$MALL communities like Madronna Island know how to keep secrets (like the matter of the beavers who will be providing our water conservation system).

Take the time one of our summer visitors—a Ph.D. in philosophy—arrived on the SS Lady Lucinda and rushed immediately into the bushes to cut himself an eight-foot cudgel.

When asked what he wanted it for, he replied, "To beat off cougars."

He was a pleasant young chap, sociably inclined, and during the next three months had long friendly sessions with almost everybody on the island (it is not possible to have a friendly session with Elinor Filibruster but that encounter was doubtless informative for a philosopher).

He visited the lighthouse, where Dan and Lena Masterson told him a great deal about the island and islanders, but never mentioned that when the foghorn is allowed to blow through its cycle twice it means that the police are coming and you better get your shot-out-of-season venison and sundry other illegalities out of sight.

He visited Jarge Gallagher, who maintains a retirement home for old machinery on the channel side. Jarge showed him his old dredge and his old war canoe and his old pile-driver and his four old bulldozers. He also showed him six long gray cylinders which the philosopher took to be old granite hot-water heaters. Jarge did not tell him they were not hot-water heaters, that they are professionally built (in Germany before the First World War) hard-liquor stills.

Jarge could truthfully say of any one of those stills, as he says of all his old machinery, "It's done its work. It's entitled to its rest." He had worked hard with those stills during the period of United States prohibition, hard enough, as I understand it, to buy the land for his rest-home. He only produced, of course. The distribution was handled through small boats, which are said to have made their deliveries to wholesalers at the border, approximately. One, at least, was never thoroughly inspected by the revenuers. It carried its stock under a false bottom upon which three pigs—always, as it happens, the same three pigs—were being transported from one island to some other. No revenuer ever got around to shovelling them out.

Captain O'Grady, our present bootlegger (government taxes forbid an impoverished island like Madronna from consuming at legal prices) has often tried to persuade Jarge to sell him the stills (and finally stole one). But Jarge will not sell. Quite a few islanders besides Captain O'Grady, and without disrespect toward Jarge, are planning to be at the auction which follows Jarge's funeral. Although the bidding will probably take place out back; Sergeant Munro of the RCMP is sure to be at the auction.

However.

The pleasant young philosopher had a happy time on Madronna and was brave as a mountain lion as long as the sun shone. But after dark, in spite of his cudgel, he grew uneasy. Quite plainly he did not like to walk home alone. So Lena Masterson walked him home. There are few vehicles on our island. Jarge walked him home. My 10-year-old twins walked him home. Even Elinor Filibruster instructed her husband to walk him home.

We all liked him, talked with him, fed him, saw him safe and happy.

But nobody ever told him that there are no cougars on Madronna Island.

THE lords of Madronna Island's feudal castle have come home again.

The castle is a dead-spar fir tree that was cut short 40 feet up by a lightning stroke many years ago. It is six feet through at the butt, and not much narrower at the top. The insects have been trying to take it to pieces for years, and might manage in a century or so. Their work has been slowed by the woodpeckers who, in pursuit of them, have drilled hundreds of holes.

The lords of the castle are a pair of osprey who return every year to reconstruct their nest on top of the spar. Osprey are such big hawks that most people think they are eagles, and they live entirely on fish. The winter winds play hob with their nest, which is largely made of sticks, and they usually have a lot of work to do before they can settle down to raising this year's family.

The instant they arrive, however, hundreds of small birds move into the woodpecker holes. You can almost see them waiting. They will squabble for a place and sometimes the contenders are not even birds that ordinarily build in holes in a tree. Upstairs the lofty ones ignore them.

But the point is, *they are upstairs*. And they will not allow anywhere in the vicinity of their castle any kind of crow. Crows eat the eggs of other birds. The osprey are not going to have their eggs eaten. Therefore, no crows. Therefore, for the fortunate residents of the desirable apartments down below, no crows either.

The osprey do not manage to preserve the peace by edict. The crows have never accepted their dominance. They try to prey on the castle. They have the impertinence, at times and in flocks, to try to steal the fish from the claws

55

of an osprey flying home. They have even been seen to get away with it. The osprey will put up with a lot. But they will not put up with a crow near their nest, and after a while they will get tired of flocks of crows trying to steal their fish.

At this point they usually work as a team. One will be flying home with a fish. A flock of crows will surround it. Suddenly, from another point of the compass, the osprey mate will appear. It will roll over in the air, snag a crow with its talons, and dive straight into the bay. Three drowned crows later, the crows give up. They're a persistent lot. You kind of have to admire them.

But the dependents of the warlords rejoice in their security. It is the mating season and they are in full song. From tiny wrens to fat robins to bush sparrows to blue jays to all the multitude of birds which we are always planning to get hold of a bird book about so we can identify them.

"The osprey are back," say the Madronna humans, glad again, because one spring they may not be.

"The osprey are back," sing their tenants.

Right around now it's the most musical highrise in Canada.

THE loggers are hurt to be called vandals. After all, they support a lot of families, their bulldozers make most of Madronna Island's trails (we would seldom be able to move a vehicle if it was left to the government), they provide the logs for the mill that makes the rough lumber for our houses, and the slashes they cut on the mountains are dressed up the following spring by eager little alders.

They were therefore delighted this spring when their work uncovered one of nature's masterpieces.

It is a great dogwood tree, growing for hundreds of years at the top of a mountain but concealed from human eyes by taller fir trees. It must have taken hundreds of years to produce a tree nine foot through the butt and 90 foot up before the first bough takes off, with four-petal blossoms as big as a dinner plate.

As soon as the white cascade was revealed, every islander who could use his feet went up for a look. But Grandpa Cuthbert can no longer use his feet.

He had been going down all winter, as the very old do sometimes, had really been holding on, we felt, for one more spring. And this was spring, and the great dogwood had been discovered on his island and it troubled him deeply that he would not see it.

It was Elwy Danson, the boss logger, who explained to the Cuthberts and the Community Club how it might be done. Elwy is six-foot four, broad in proportion, young and powerful. "We could take him up in the government truck to the bottom of the cut," he said. "Then the crew could strap a chair to my back and harness Gramp to the chair and I could take him the rest of the way on the bulldozer." It was agreed that the old man should make his own decision.

"It'd be a chance," Elwy told him. "You mightn't make it up, Gramp, and you mightn't make it down. But you *might* see the big dogwood."

"I'd thank you for the back, Elwy," said Gramp. And that night his daughter-in-law got him early to bed and the next morning the whole island came to convoy him up the mountain. Even Mildred Stonehenge, who is 91 to his 89 and has entertained similar ambitions to claim the first grave in the new cemetery (though not to die first; remember, this kind of daydreaming requires that the other be lost at sea).

We got him safely to the bottom of the cut, but it was a frail bundle of old bones that the loggers strapped to Elwy's back, a frail old bundle with the blaze of spring in its eyes. Elwy took that bulldozer up the mountain like a baby carriage. He brought Grandpa to the foot of the tree, to see its girth, and across to the cliff edge so that he could measure its height and print on his eyes the vast fountain of its bloom. A logger spurred his way up the trunk, and brought Grandpa a blossom. It filled his lap and spilled over.

Grandpa's hand touched the great blossom, his eyes lifted to the great tree.

"I have seen," he said reverently, "the biggest dogwood in the world."

It was a tender trip the bulldozer made to the bottom of the cut, and half-way there Elwy cut the engine and turned his head to listen a moment to the old man. Then he brought the bulldozer down beside the government truck.

The loggers unstrapped an empty old bundle of bones from Elwy's back. Grandpa Cuthbert had gone somewhere else to look for bigger dogwood trees.

"He asked me," said Elwy carefully, "to tell Mildred that he'd meet her in the graveyard."

58

P EOPLE in these waters have been reporting sightings lately. Not of Unidentified Flying Objects but of Little Penguins.

Richard James and I saw one, sitting on a log in the middle of the channel. Richard, who is Madronna Island's resident freelance writer and believes he is a realist, swept on past. A hundred yards further on he made an abrupt U-turn for which I was prepared (Richard is in fact a romantic) and roared back. Just before we reached his log the little penguin dived, and Richard bent his propeller on the log.

"But it was a little penguin!" he asserted, rowing home.

There have been reports from more reliable observers. Tugboat operators, log boomers, fishermen, Indians and the captain of a Japanese freighter have all reported little penguins. The captain of the Japanese freighter presented the Madronna school children who had stopped his ship with four new swear words (Japanese) for their profanity collection before relenting and telling them about little penguins. Stopping ships and asking what cargo they are carrying where is a learning process recently urged upon the children by our teacher, Mrs. Gathercole.

The Japanese captain saw two little penguins on the shore of Cooper Island. They were shuffling a pebble from the foot of the one to the foot of the other.

For every observer of a little penguin there has been a scoffer, usually armed with a bird book, who says that what we saw was a duck or a diver or a mudhen or some other feathered aquatic: Just look at this picture! The problem for sanity is that the picture never looks like what we saw, which was a little penguin.

It is the other problem for sanity that has engaged the attention of the mainland university ornithologist who often visits Madronna. We are well up in the northern hemisphere, where there are no penguins.

So when the lighthouse keeper, tying up at the government wharf, remarked that Jim Carpenter, the road foreman, *had* a little penguin, Richard dived for the phone and told the ornithologist to take a plane right up. "Jim took him off an eagle," said the lighthouse keeper. "He'd been mauled a bit." "What did he look like?" asked Richard. "Like a little penguin," said the lighthouse keeper.

We got to the beach where Jim Carpenter was straightening a curve in the trail just as the ornithologist's float plane put down. The ornithologist, who was a little over-excited, fell into the water getting out. "Where's the penguin?" he demanded, putting sanity behind him. "Over under the lip of that rock," said Jim, getting on with his road building.

We rushed over to the rock. No penguin. No nothing.

"I guess," said Jim, when we rushed back to him, "that he got well enough to take off on his own. He wasn't much hurt. The eagle didn't have a good grip of him or he wouldn't have dropped him when I yelled. I just smoothed him down a bit and put him where the eagle couldn't get at him. Last time I looked he was tidying his feathers, the way they do in the zoo."

"You should have hung onto him," screamed the ornithologist.

"Now then," said Jim reproachfully. "You know a wild thing's best left to cure itself, if it's not hurt too bad."

We all averted our gaze respectfully. The ornithologist was blubbering.

After a long pause he asked, "What did he look like?"

"Like a little penguin," said Jim.

NINETY-TWO candles, and Mildred Stonehenge got them all out with one good long blast. Which ought to have been surprising, because the tears were still running down her cheeks in tribute to the rendition of *her* song, I Don't Want to Play in Your Yard. But Mildred has a good pair of bellows.

With the assistance of a large number of honorary Madronna Islanders, the Madronna school children were last Friday night able to sing the right words and the Madronna rock band (gone folk for the night) to play the right music to Mildred's first favorite. They will present her second favorite, Two Little Girls in Blue—it turned out she had mixed up two songs in her remembering—for her ninety-third birthday.

Mildred was so touched by the kindness of so many that she decided to do a kindness herself. She decided to let Elinor Filibruster perform her toreador dance at the birthday party. This was not viewed as a kindness by 55 of the 57 residents of Madronna. Mrs. Gathercole, the school teacher, had refused to have Elinor's dance at the Christmas concert, Charlie Jo at the New Year's see-in and Mrs. Carpenter at the Easter at-home for other islands. It was not that we dislike Elinor, although we do. It was that we feared her dance would be an acute embarrassment. Mildred said we should endure for compassion's sake.

Elinor had been rehearsing the dance for a year. She was the toreador in a tight black body stocking ("And those 42-inch hips!" as Mrs. Carpenter comments from time to time), and a scarlet-lined black cape. The rear of the bull was her husband, who is short, and the head was Irwin Hoffstater, who is tall and a little wanting. These were the only two islanders who would submit to Elinor's arbitrary

61

hours of rehearsal. Hours and hours of them, for months and months; Elinor's husband with his hands on Irwin's shoulders so that they would be properly synchronized, getting the steps so much by heart that they tended, when juxtaposed, to break into them automatically even on off-duty occasions.

The bull had not been able to practice in costume, because the bull costume had been a horse for Christmas and a donkey for Easter and the costume committee—Mrs. Carpenter—had not got around to whipping up a bull's head until the afternoon of the evening of Mildred's party.

The rock band struck up its version of the toreador waltz, the toreador bounded on stage, and here came the bull. Backwards.

But faithful. It charged the toreador's scarlet cape, rump first. It snorted, from the wrong end. After that the sound of both band and bull were lost in audience reaction. The dance went on. Elinor is not an adjustable person. She never thought to stop the performance and reverse the dirty work (Elwy Danson says Richard James, Richard James says Elwy Danson) of whoever had suited up the bull. She just went on dancing and the bull went on charging, rump first.

We laughed until we couldn't breathe, and Mrs. Carpenter and I had to help Mildred to the back porch or she might, literally, have died laughing. At which point Elinor broke her wooden sword over the bull and tore raging out of the hall.

Mr. Carpenter, justice of the peace, rushed to the rescue of her husband. "We'll have to take the poor little fellow into protective custody," he said.

"Virtue," said Mildred, getting her breath back but still clutching her side, "is its own reward."

UNLESS you are willing to go into a permanent state of siege it is better to decide, on Madronna Island, that you like nature rough. There *are* islanders who have beautiful formal gardens. They are surrounded by eight to 10 foot fences, to keep out the deer.

The deer in the vicinity of Hobart Coyne and Bert Walshe can jump only eight feet. The deer in the vicinity of the Robertsons and the Bateses are a better breed, they can jump 10 feet. You can be opposed to your deer removing the bark from young fruit trees, but you don't run them down.

The deer are very cosmopolitan in their eating habits. What they don't eat they walk on. This is why most of us have decided that a beautiful island, dressed up with mountains and sea, doesn't really need nasturtiums.

On the other hand, we are all strongly in favor of vegetable gardens. So are the deer and raccoons. No vacuum cleaner was ever as efficient as a deer picking peas. He can take every pod in two rows as he walks at a gentle pace—chivvied from behind by the brooms of the owners—between the rows. He prefers really young peas, pods and all, so if you want the peas for yourself there is nothing for it but a fence.

No fence will stop coons.

The only way to stop coons is to lid with wire that part of the garden which will attract their attention, and put a padlock on the door that opens into it. Bert Walshe says even this won't stop his coons. They picked his padlock.

Coons are choosy about what they will eat. Bert says what they like best for the main course is one of his chickens. Then for dessert they like to walk along his fence and pick the raspberries from his raspberry canes.

At our place we have a fence around the vegetable garden for the deer and a dog for the coons. A little dog won't do. The coons would take him apart and hang his pelt to the back door. On the other hand, we did not want a really big dog, like a malamute we were offered, because a dog that size could take a coon apart and hang *his* pelt. So we have Tippy, who is about the right size: both he and the coon would have second thoughts about paw-to-paw combat. Whenever he thinks he hears coons in the garden or orchard, which is a good deal too often for uneasy sleepers, he dashes out through his own special little door and makes very loud and challenging sounds.

Last evening Tippy treed a coon. It was a very small coon, about 12 inches long not counting tail, but very truculent. It took the family, me poking with a broom from below, the twins pushing with leather-gloved hands up top, to get him sealed in a box. Then the problem arose.

The island rule is that a coon actually caught stealing is shot and made into a coonskin hat. But, as the twins pointed out, he wasn't big enough to make a hat. On the other hand it would be socially destructive with their peer group to admit that they had let a thieving coon go.

Fortunately our justice of the peace, Mr. Carpenter, arrived in time to deliver the verdict. The coon, he argued, was in the orchard, which made the case against him bad. But, for the defence, he had been up the tree which was apple but did not yet have apples, and not down among the strawberries at its foot. "I think," said Mr. Carpenter, "it would be fair if you gave him a 24-hour start and then went after him."

The twins will start hunting him tonight.

RICHARD James, our resident freelance writer, has commended himself to Jim Carpenter by helping him stage mock courts. Mr. Carpenter, in addition to being the justice of the peace on Madronna Island, is the magistrate. This has not so far come to public attention because he has always managed to settle his cases out of court.

Mr. Carpenter's desire to settle cases out of court is partially in deference to the Almighty's prerogative in matters of judgment. But he is also concerned that he might not cut quite the right figure on the Bench.

There are few on the island who can coach him in the proper dignities, since those who have been in the courts have usually been in them on the mainland, on drunk charges (or theft in the case of Captain O'Grady), and have not been in a condition to observe the amenities. Mr. Carpenter thought a writer who had been a police court reporter ought to know.

The first time they used Irwin for the accused. Irwin is not very bright but he is obliging.

"Irwin Hoffstater," intoned Richard, in the role of court clerk, "you are charged that on the second day of April, in the year 1978, in the county of Butterfield, in contravention of Section 30, Subsection 3(a) of the Criminal Code, you did with felonious intent commit an aggravated assault, to wit, that you did hit Joseph Smith on the back of the head. How do you plead, guilty or not guilty?"

"Guilty," said Irwin promptly.

"You can't plead guilty," objected Mr. Carpenter, "because that would end the trial and I need the practice. Plead not guilty."

"But I hit him."

"You couldn't have hit him. You don't know him. He

doesn't exist.''

"I hit Ray Badger. I hit him on the back of the head with a boat hook.''

"Why did you hit Ray Badger?'' demanded Mrs. Carpenter.

"He was robbing my crab pots.''

"Then plead not guilty,'' suggested Richard helpfully. "I'll be your defence lawyer and argue that Ray Badger's theft served as provocation.''

"I opened the whole back of his head,'' said Irwin, with relish. "Old Doc Filbert had to put in 11 stitches. You should of heard Ray holler. I had to sit on his back and hold his head by the ears while the Doc was stitching.''

"James,'' demanded Mrs. Carpenter, "did you know anything about this?''

"Of course not,'' said Mr. Carpenter. "The Doc wouldn't tell me because he'd be afraid I might have to take official notice and call in Sergeant Munro.''

"And there has been no complaint from the victim,'' said Richard repressively. "Are the stitches out, Irwin?''

"Last Tuesday,'' said Irwin.

"Well then,'' said Richard, "how do you plead? Guilty or not guilty?''

"Guilty!'' said Irwin, proudly.

Mr. Carpenter and Richard decided it would be easier to try Ray Badger, in absentia, for robbing crab pots. And in the study, where they wouldn't be interrupted.

"I have never,'' said Mrs. Carpenter, "understood the logic of the male mind.''

M ADRONNA Island has never understood the international balance of payments, but it understands the principle all right. The principle is to get more off-island money onto the island than islanders spend off the island.

Charlie Jo fathomed one idea when he was under the tutelage of the Brothers in an Indian residential school and had averaged 87 per cent and did not choose to go on to university. Government grants. For two years now he has been able to get grants (with the aid of the Community Club) to keep the older teenagers of the island employed during the summer. His projects are basically sound, in that they improve the island—a logger-ruined stream cleaned up so that the salmon will return to spawn; a lake basin cleared to become a reservoir for a beaver-constructed water-conservation system.

Of course, a government grant may not be forthcoming next year, but Charlie will worry about that then.

The Small Spirit also puts money into teenage pockets. It is Madronna's rock (and, when necessary, folk) band. The Small Spirit plays for free on Madronna, but off Madronna it takes as much as it can get, when it feels like playing, that is. Charlie is the only Indian in the band, but the others have all dyed their hair black and find it easy to adopt Charlie's philosophy, which is that if you want to go to the canoe races instead of playing for the Legion dance on Cooper Island, you go to the canoe races. True, this makes the Cooper Legion mad as hell, but what can they do about it? Nobody has been able to organize a band on Cooper. As Charlie says, they just don't understand the powers of a monopoly.

The more serious unemployment problem is among the younger teenagers and the children. While the adults of the island usually make enough one way and another to pay the store bill (and the Carpenters are very understanding when they don't), I expect most of the incomes on this island are below what the mainland would call the poverty level. So there are no regular allowances for children. The children, on the other hand, are as greedy for money as children anywhere.

Actually they could make money by cutting firewood for summer visitors, but that would offend against island mores. This is a loggers' island, and people who take down trees averaging four foot through the butt do not fiddle with firesticks, except for themselves, of course. Would you have the children demean themselves?

This year Charlie Jo has got around the social problem. Clearing the basin for the new lake means taking out a number of big trees and a lot of small ones. The older teenagers cut the big stuff into stove lengths and leave the rest whole. The younger teenagers and children have been allowed, after a solemn conference, to make their contribution to Madronna's lake by cutting the total fell into sizes that can be readily removed. Into firewood, that is. Mr. Carpenter has put up a sign in the store advertising firewood for sale (at rather more than mainland prices). Delivery is made by the government truck (which the government, Mr. Carpenter says, doesn't need to know about), and the children do the loading and unloading.

"It's not what you do," said Charlie Jo to Mr. Carpenter, as they observed the laboring children (who will be rich as Croesus), "but what you see yourself to be doing."

RICHARD James, our resident freelance writer, sat on the kitchen counter of the community hall and described the impossible. "It's steel," he said, "and it's got two ovens and it was new last fall and the boss logger over at Tarra is selling it cheap because he's going up coast."

"What's cheap?" asked Mrs. Carpenter. "Fifty dollars." "They'd never go for it,"said Mrs. Carpenter bitterly.

"The men have been drying their boots in the oven of this one again," said Flo Davis resignedly, "and they left the door open and it's stinking of mice-urine." Which means scouring it out with steel wool and yellow soap and heating it slightly and scouring and heating and scouring and so on until the stink is gone. Because a fire in a mice-urined stove to make the coffee for the bridge club that night would drive the club into the bushes. "You'd better step down to the store for some more steel wool," Mrs. Carpenter told me. And then she said, "But wait. There's a hockey game."

The stove at the community hall is a sore point between male and female members of the Community Club. It is always a discard, thrown out by some island family because it simply won't cook any more. At the emergency meeting invariably called to discuss the matter the women say, "But look, we have to cook for 50 people on this stove." And the men say, "But you can cook everything else at home and it makes splendid coffee." And the women all vote for a new stove and the men win for the old one because the bachelors give them the balance of power.

"You haven't joined the Community Club yet, have you?" Mrs. Carpenter asked me. "You're joining now. Richard, arrange to pick up all the women on the Channel

69

side. Some of the men will be staying home to listen to the hockey game. Have Elinor Filibruster bring her husband, because he's this year's president and we'll need him to convene the emergency meeting. I'll send Mr. Carpenter for the June Harbor vote but I'll have to fix it so he can't pick up old Lester or old Robbie. They're very anti-stove. And Richard, stand by Irwin at the vote"—Irwin isn't too smart—"and shove up his hand for the right side."

So that night the bridge club, slightly more female than usual, gathered sharp at seven (hockey game safely on but old Lester and old Robbie present, having walked). The stove was carefully laid, with a cup of kerosene for the last moment.

"I'm sorry to have to ask you to touch the match to it," Mrs. Carpenter told me. "But you're the only woman on the island who'd be fool enough to do it with the oven in that condition."

Have you ever smelled a mice-urined stove in full blast? It is like very bad meat, much multiplied and penetrating. By the middle of the first rubber the bridge club had to retreat to the porch. As the guilty party I was able to burst into tears (scent not sentiment) and sob about how maybe I could replace the stove with the stove from Tarra. Elinor Filibruster commanded her husband to convene an emergency meeting of the Community Club which, weeping (you would have to smell it to believe it), he did. Mr. Carpenter was so sorry for me he moved, seconded by Elinor, that the Community Club purchase the Tarra stove. Passed.

After that we retired, still weeping, to the Carpenters' kitchen at the store for coffee and hot cinnamon buns. But old Lester and old Robbie went home mad. They said it was a set up. They went separated, because they're not speaking, but they were united in indignation and democracy.

DOE Kelly comes in once a week to clean my house. She is delicate about it, she comes when she knows I'll be up the mountain cutting greens. At first I didn't know who was responsible for the unusual spic-and-spanness. But then Mrs. Carpenter up at the store told me. She knows everything. So I sought out Doe and thanked her and tried to bring up, as delicately as she had done the work, the matter of payment.

"No," said Doe, with absolute finality. "You can't afford it. I love tucking into a dirty house." She smiled on me. "We islanders," she said, "know that a writer can't help being dirty."

We islanders are also damn accurate. But how does one repay a favor of that size? Or the favor of Irwin Hoffstater, who just happened to turn up one other day while I was up the mountain and dug my vegetable garden? And then was there the first thing next morning with a string of pegs to help me put in the seeds? So deep for the carrots and lettuce, so much deeper for the peas and beans, with hills for the potatoes and the squash. Mysteriously instructed in these things, for Irwin is not very bright, as he is also instructed in the matter of water carriers.

He fixed our whole family up with water carriers this week.

The people who own this house brought in water from a spring that tends to run dry in the summer, and we store drinking water in old oil drums that have been steamed out. But there is always the chance that the spring will run dry and the rain will not fall and that we will be forced back on a brackish well. And the vegetable garden, of course, must always drink brackish water. It must be carried, and that is literally a back-breaking job. Unless you have one of

71

Irwin's water carriers.

He whipped them up out of laths he found in the woodshed. You make a rectangle, big or small, depending on the size of who will be carrying the water, and how long his stride and his arms are. The first two were for the twins, Michael and Judy, who are 10, but Dorene, who is four, insisted on having one, too.

You fill two buckets with water and set them apart on the ground. The water carrier is laid on top of them, with the handles of the buckets outside the laths. You then step inside the rectangle, pick up the buckets with their handles resting against the lath sides, and waltz away as though you were carrying feathers.

There were two district engineers up at the Carpenters' when we went along to demonstrate Irwin's water carriers, and at first they were very condescending. They said the effect was purely psychological, and that all the carriers did was hold the buckets away from your legs so you wouldn't get slopped.

But then they tried mine and found that, indeed, it made the buckets lighter. Unbelievably lighter, so that not being strong at all you can walk for a mile carrying two full-sized buckets full of water. It made the engineers very cross. We left them arguing about third-class levers and fulcrums and promising to phone the university in the morning.

But if I were you, and had to carry water at my summer place, I'd forget about universities and just make one of Irwin's water carriers. All it takes is two short laths and two longer laths and two nails for each corner. And it works.

J UST put a gallon of Javex on the account," Charlie Jo explained, coming through from the Carpenters' store into the Carpenters' kitchen. "The Brothers are coming."

"Now Charlie," said Mrs. Carpenter, "I told you the next time the Brothers came I'd help Mary clean up the boat. It's not fair always to make the Brothers work for their holiday. Those are hot cinnamon buns under that tea towel. Help yourself."

Charlie helped himself to four buns. He is 18, Indian, and lives on a 30-foot boat with his grandmother, granfather, mother, father, younger brother and younger sister. Their standards of hygiene are about on a level with mine, but there's a stronger smell of fish.

"The Brothers," said Charlie, "don't work for their holiday. They work for their souls. It is properly humbling for them to scrub out an Indian fishboat. We like having them in spite of the Javex. Brother Mark," he told Mr. Carpenter, "can hardly wait to get at that midden Elwy Danson put his bulldozer through."

"It was careless of Elwy," said Mr. Carpenter. "I told him I was sure there was a midden there. Professor Sortisio is going to be angry."

"Elwy didn't do it for Professor Sortisio," said Charlie. "He did it for Brother Mark. The professor prefers to unearth my ancestors with a feather duster. Brother Mark likes them broadside, like a department store."

"He won't like this one that way," said Mr. Carpenter. "I don't think it's a kitchen midden. There's the skeleton of a child."

"High enough up to belong to the Christian era?" asked Charlie, interested. "That would please Brother John. He could get Father Baker and rebury it with proper Christian

73

rites.''

"Charlie," said Mrs. Carpenter severely, "stop be-
having like a teenager. But of course you are a teenager. I
think you're still growing. Jim"—to Mr. Carpenter—
"measure him against his mark by the door. I think he's
put on at least an inch.''

Charlie proved to be an inch and a quarter past his last
mark.

"Six foot one," said Mr. Carpenter. "They can't be your
ancestors in the middens. All the ones we've uncovered are
real small, four or five feet.''

"So were your ancestors at the Battle of Agincourt,"
said Charlie, snaffling another bun. "It's all this over-
feeding that's done it.''

"Now that's what I mean," said Mrs. Carpenter.
"You're a well educated boy because of the Brothers and
you make fun of their religion.''

"Fun?" said Charlie, raising his eyebrows. "I have
every respect for the Christian ethic. I merely reject the
Christian faith.''

"Well, tomorrow you'd better not reject a Christian
spade. We're going to collect that poor little skeleton and
bury it in the graveyard. And you're not to tease Brother
John.''

"You are really," said Charlie, "depriving Brother John
of a meaningful religious experience.''

"No respect," said Mrs. Carpenter, "that's what
troubles me. No respect.''

Charlie collected his gallon of Javex and went through
the door. Then he put his head back round it. "I have the
utmost respect for you, Mrs. Carpenter," he said, grinning. "When you're coming to our boat I wash our whole
table. When you're coming"—he looked at me—"I don't
wash it at all, because you're a pig, like us. But when Elinor
Filibruster comes I wash exactly one quarter and sit her at
it so she can think, 'These dirty Indians!' Now *that's*
disrespect.''

"Yes," said Mrs. Carpenter soberly. "It is.''

CAPTAIN O'Grady and old Lester Cholmondeley (known to the islanders as Les Chumley) are always happy to sample each half-bottle of liquor we beachcomb on the Channel side so that we can be sure that we will not be poisoning our summer guests.

The bottles are always half-full and securely corked. Presumably those that are full go straight to the bottom and those that are insecurely corked fill up with sea water and do the same thing. But it is amazing how many part bottles of scotch, rum, rye, bourbon, brandy and every sort of liqueur come floating in. Almost no wine, however. It has left us curious about the nature of shipboard parties.

Whatever the original source, these contributions from the sea give a nice international flavor to the drinks we serve our paying guests. They are on the house, which is unusual and causes our guests to wonder out loud how we can do it at the price.

The sea explains part of it (except, of course, that we do not explain it). Then there is Captain O'Grady's gin which if flavored with juniper we serve from gin bottles, and if unflavored from vodka bottles. The Captain's gin is $8 a gallon. We make our own blackberry wine.

Our guests are mainly academics (Richard James, our resident freelance writer, having pointed out that only academics would be fools enough to pay good prices for space in our primitive hostels—no electric light and usually no running water). Some of them last only a day or two before succumbing to the terrors of rural silence and renting a small boat to get back to civilization. But if we can shepherd them through that first touchy period, they will settle down happily to gathering their own food from the sea and the mountains, helping us to pick greenery for the mainland florists and educating our children.

It is true that the political scientist at my place entertains the grossest contempt for the political scientist at Mrs. Cuthbert's, thus acquainting the children with the fact that there can be dissension in academe, but he and my historian can sit on the front porch and talk for hours. They are in no way inhibited by having half a dozen of the island youth scattered around their feet. In fact, take a professor away from his campus, set him down before a lot of ignorant but eager listeners, and it is against his nature not to expound. As the young in this case do not realize that they are being taught they do not object to learning.

They are perhaps happiest with the astronomer who lies out on the beach with them and tells them which stars are where (complete with myths), the anthropologist who has shown them the proper method of excavating a midden, and the marine biologist who tells them the right names for the marine creatures with which they are already well acquainted on an informal basis.

The chemist would undoubtedly like to visit Captain O'Grady's still, but he will not be invited.

There are times when I feel a little guilty, especially when they thank me so heartily for such a wonderful and inexpensive holiday, and especially with the historian. He would be delighted to buy up gallons and gallons of the captain's gin and take it home. But you can't trust professors. They talk. They can't help talking. It's a professional affliction.

And the island could not possibly run the risk of the secret of the Captain's gin reaching the ears of Police Sergeant Munro.

I T was about 3:30 in the afternoon when the eagle dived in front of Richard James' boat and took the dogfish shark. Took it and rose in flight perhaps eight feet and then was heeled over by its weight—it was a huge dogfish—and brought down to the sea and the great battle.

In the first hour the eagle made it into brief flight perhaps half a dozen times but each time the weight of the dogfish bore it down and the fight skated in undiminished passion across acres of ocean calm. The eagle would not let go.

Richard had throttled his boat down after the first plunge and he followed the two wild things as they pitted their power against each other. "Why won't he let go?" he said anxiously after a while, and brought an oar up beside him and the boat in as close as possible. "Here, take the wheel," he said to me. "Run us almost on top of them." And I did and he tried to strike at the dogfish under the water, but one of the eagle's wings hurled the oar out of his hand and the feathers and scales flashed away from us.

We were joined after a while by Elwy Danson in his boat and Charlie Jo in his. "You, Elwy," called Richard, "can you come in on them from the right while I come in from the left? And we'll try to get that dogfish." "It's their fight," shouted Charlie Jo.

But the two white men did not hear him. They came in carefully on the seethe of feathers, their oars poised for the chop. The great wings of the eagle—they did not want to hurt the eagle—made their attack too distant. They were not sure that they had been able to hit the dogfish at all. The eagle's eyes gleamed fiercely, we could see the blood under his talons. His embattled wings took the war away from us.

It was now nearly five o'clock.

"Perhaps he can't let go," said Richard, rather desperately. "Perhaps his talons are locked."

"We've all seen an eagle drop its prey," said Charlie Jo. "He doesn't want to let go."

"But he will die."

"At the end of a great battle," said Charlie Jo.

"Take the wheel," said Richard to me again, "and work us close." He ripped off his shirt, caught a coil of rope and tied one end to a hold on the boat and the other around his body under his arms. He grabbed a knife. "I'm going to get that dogfish from underneath," he said, and was over the side.

"No!" shouted Charlie Jo. He brought his boat hard against Richard's and leaped aboard. He hauled on the rope, dragging Richard back. What surfaced was a body shimmering with blood. "There are thousands of dogfish just underneath," whispered Richard. "Yes," said Charlie Jo, "they have slashed you with their fins." He pulled off his shirt and started tearing it and Richard's into strips. "Yours, too," he said to Elwy and me. He wrapped Richard tightly in the strips, like a mummy. "It will hold the bleeding till we get you to hospital," he told Richard. "You will be all right. Like a waffle for a while, but they did not get your eyes." He pushed his own boat off. "Elwy, will you take this in tow?"

"The eagle," said Richard, who might have been crying, or it might have been drops from the sea. "My friend," said Charlie, laying a hand across the friend's eyes. The strips of shirt were reddening. "Blood of the lamb," said Charlie, and gunned the motor.

It was nearly six o'clock, Elwy told us later, when the dogfish shark dragged the eagle under and the battle was lost.

"Or won," said Charlie Jo.

THE school exercises were enlivened last Friday by the presence of Pete, the baby seal.

Pete turned up in June Harbor this spring without a mother. The school stands at the head of June Harbor. The Madronna Island school children and Pete were buddies at the first shake of a flipper. Pete doesn't really seem to miss his mother, but he is so fond of company that the children have been going down even Saturdays and Sundays to make sure he has it.

The Madronna adults were not particularly aware of Pete's presence until he scared the children by becoming ill after a lunch of cheese sandwiches, chocolate cake, buns, cold pancakes, peanut brittle, watercress and bubble gum. Fearing for his health they summoned Doc Filbert, who summoned old Robbie Robinson, a retired commercial fisherman.

Robbie said the children were positively not to feed Pete human food. Hadn't they heard on the radio about the seal in a mainland zoo who died with a stomach full of hot dogs? He would drop off a bucket a day of live herring for Pete, although personally he couldn't see what they wanted with a seal, just varmints they were, cutting down on the salmon catch.

With old Robbie's herring, the children taught Pete to balance a ball on his nose, take objects out of their pockets and count up to three in clam shells. That is, they may have, or Pete may have picked it up for himself.

He very early learned what the school bell meant, and would gallumph for the path that leads up the cliff to the schoolhouse. Sending one of the older students out to take Pete back to his sea became a usual chore for Mrs. Gathercole, the teacher.

The school's pet pig, Elinor, who will be going home with the Bateses for the holidays, was safely penned in the schoolyard during the school exercises. But Pete was there. Mrs. Gathercole had instructed two of the boys to provide a bucket of salt water and sponges so his coat wouldn't get dry (bad for a seal, says old Robbie).

The purpose of the exercises is to permit all of the 12 students to show off their learning and Mrs. Gathercole to show off her teaching. The whole island was there and the whole island was serious: for Madronna it is the community taking a solemn look at the performance of the school.

Good performance, too. While a young Danson recited the times table (up to 20 times 20—Mrs. Gathercole believes in getting back to basics), Pete laid one, two, three school books at his feet. While a young Bates recited her own poem about a goldfinch on a thistle flower, Pete removed from her pocket a fishline, two sinkers, a fishhook bedded in cork and a copy of the poem (in case she forgot).

When the poem was rewarded with a thunder of applause, old Robbie cut through the thunder to demand, "Who's going to look after that seal while you're all on holidays? You can't take *him* home with you, and the summer people will fill him up with junk and kill him."

It was a serious point, certainly, which disrupted the exercises until old Robbie volunteered to spend the summer hanging around June Harbor (he lives just behind) to look out for summer visitors. After that a slightly older Bates recited the powers the provinces *ought* to have under the BNA Act (Mrs. Gathercole is a strong provincialist).

So if you sail up a deep, quiet island harbor this summer and meet a friendly young seal capering on the beach, don't feed him macaroons. Or a fierce white-haired old man will come out of the bushes and get you.

P EOPLE who are brought up in boats have a particular way of moving in them that is rather beautiful. The small child who is bringing a dinghy alongside the wharf ships his oars as unconsciously as he plants his feet and handles his body for balance. A big, stout woman like Mrs. Carpenter, whom you would expect to swamp the thing, moves as casually as if she were crossing her kitchen floor.

Actually, it was Mrs. Carpenter, getting out of Dan Potter's boat at his float in June Harbor a couple of summers ago, who first concentrated my attention on this aspect of the islands. She was being gracious to Dan Potter, whom she had dragooned into transporting us from the government wharf and who was being his usual uncouth self. We stood on his float for a minute while she congratulated him on his wood pile, which he keeps five years ahead and of which he never gives a stick to anybody. And then we were treated to a really superlative demonstration of boat-plus-human equalling single entity.

Charlie Jo, who was 16 then, came running all out down the float, leaped into Dan's boat without breaking stride or causing it to more than tremble, gunned it to life and went roaring down the harbor.

Leaving Dan roaring on the dock. Now that was a superlative demonstration, too, of its sort. Dan has always been a mean man (wore out most of the mainland before he inflicted himself on Madronna) but he is not generally counted a fluent man. A mistake. He used all the profanity and obscenity we had ever heard and some we hadn't (it took us three weeks to find out what one word meant, it wasn't in the dictionary).

To be absolutely fair to him, he did not attack Charlie as an Indian. Dan's discrimination is larger than that. He hates the whole human race and, more particularly and especially, the young of the human race.

He hadn't finished when he had to repeat himself, because Charlie Jo was coming back. Charlie cut the engine when the boat was about 50 feet out and let its way bring it in (that's what I mean, boat-born people can judge that sort of thing to the inch). Charlie's face, lifted to the ranting on the float, wore the perfect politeness impressed upon it (for use with elders) by the Brothers. He brought the boat alongside the float like a fish.

"All right, you kids," he said, "you can get out now."

And up from the hidden bow rose two drenched nine-year-olds, the son and the daughter of a couple of summer families.

"Lena called the Jessups from the lighthouse," explained Charlie. "She got these two, on a home-made raft, in her glasses, and the lighthouse boat was out. The tide was taking them. You'd better get along home now," he told the two, "and I think Mr. Carpenter will be around to talk to your parents about home-made rafts."

Poor Dan Potter.

"It would have been kinder," said Mrs. Carpenter, as he shambled wordless, broken, up the float, "to tell him why you needed his boat."

"Well," said Charlie, "Lena said the raft was breaking up, so there wasn't much time. And after I'd fished them out and we were coming home,"—he grinned—"it seemed too good a chance to waste. So I had the kids hunker down in the bow."

"You're a bad boy," said Mrs. Carpenter, hugging him. "Now we'd better make sure those children get home."

When I mentioned the beauty of the performance, neither Mrs. Carpenter nor Charlie knew what I was talking about. They're boat people.

"MR. CARPENTER," said Mrs. Carpenter, "doesn't believe there was just one Noah. He thinks there were a lot. He thinks they were sensible men who looked up at the sky after it had been raining and raining and all of a sudden thought, 'It's raining too damn much.'

"So then they built a raft. And they put the wife and kids on it, and the hens and a cock, and a sow and a boar. Or with some it would be a couple of goats and some geese. And seed grain, of course. And then they rode it out. He thinks Noah made it into the Bible because he turned it into a good story that grew."

The subject arose while Lettie Danson and Mrs. Carpenter and I were listing a new batch of books for the Madronna Island library. The library had been the idea of Richard James, our resident freelance writer. He felt uneasy because there was no place you could go and browse among books, so he brought it up at the Community Club and it was moved by Richard, seconded by Mr. Carpenter, that the men would build an addition to the hall to be called the library and the women would canvass everyone on the island, and all visitors, for contributions.

Madronna is not what anybody would call an intellectual island. Most of its citizens don't read very much, except catalogues. But they respect books, much as they respect the chapel. That is, they keep the books dusted and they keep the roof of the chapel sound, but they don't spend a great deal of time inside either.

The books donated by the islanders, therefore, tended to be of two sorts. The first lot was old, obviously handed down. These consisted of such items as complete editions of Shakespeare and Charles Dickens, large illustrated copies of the Bible full of rather terrible portraits of God, and no fewer than six early editions of Mrs. Beeton's Cook Book. The other lot of books donated by the islanders consisted of encyclopedias and dictionaries.

The islanders have built up virtually no resistance to the hard sales pitch. When a salesman arrives—which is fortunately infrequently—they go down before him like trees before a bulldozer. Whether he ever collects more than the downpayment, I wouldn't be prepared to say. It was moved by Richard, seconded by Mr. Carpenter, that Richard be appointed a committee of one to sell the duplicates and purchase modern books of reference.

For lighter reading material we depend mainly upon the summer visitors, who are so anxious to promote our educational project that they always leave their paperbacks behind.

Thus it was that Mrs. Carpenter came to read *On the Beach,* by Nevil Shute, and get around to Noah.

On the Beach, as you doubtless remember, is about the last months of humanity on earth, after the nuclear war has been fought to a finish in the northern hemisphere, and the southern hemisphere—chiefly Australia—is simply sitting and waiting for inevitable radioactive death.

"And that," said Mrs. Carpenter firmly, "is where Mr. Shute got it all wrong. They wouldn't have sat and waited. They would have been working out a million ways to beat those clouds of radioactive dust. Like Noah. They would each have been figuring that maybe it was going to get everybody else, but it wasn't going to get HER."

"But what could they have done?" I asked. "The scientists..."

"I don't know what they could have done in Australia," said Mrs. Carpenter. "But here, we made popcorn."

I T was during the Cuban nuclear crisis, Mrs. Carpenter said, that Madronna, like Noah, decided to save itself.

Nobody on the island had noticed that there was a crisis. But the morning it began a visiting writer arrived with a newspaper and a burden of anxiety. He was terribly afraid the balloon was going up.

Nobody listened to him. Nobody listened to the radio either. Nobody does, on Madronna, until after supper. After supper, however, the writer fretted Mr. Carpenter into it and what Mr. Carpenter heard convinced him, like Noah, that it was raining too damn much.

He went straight to the phone and dialed the three shorts and two longs that summon Harry Cuthbert.

"Carpenter, Harry," he said. "Don't much like the sound of the news..."

"No. Well, remember we talked of putting that spring into the tunnel. I'll send Irwin over with a couple hundred feet of pipe, and call some of the others. You could take the water where it comes out of the rock, and then pack the join with about six feet of earth. We don't want contamination. Better trench a good three feet for the pipe. That young buck still feeding with your cows?...

"Good. Better get him in the barn. I'll have Danson round up that doe's been hanging around his place. If it comes to it, deer would probably be more useful than cattle. Better foragers. Be there as soon as I can."

Below the Cuthberts' is an abandoned mining tunnel. Not a very big tunnel—Mr. Carpenter has to stoop to walk it—but punched a couple of hundred yards through hard rock and as durable as the mountain above it.

If they did start dropping nuclear bombs, Mr. Carpenter intended to put the whole of Madronna in that tunnel, with an assortment of animals and foodstuffs. There would be safe water from the spring. There would be safe air, if they could figure out a filter. There would, short of a direct hit, be a chance.

They were all very busy that night and the next day. In the end, Mrs. Carpenter told us, all of the islanders but the Mastersons, who had to stand by the lighthouse, and Jarge Gallagher who elected to go up with his retired machines, were gathered in the community hall. In the Cuthbert barn were the buck and the doe, two sows and a boar, cows and bull, banty hens and cock, ordinary hens and cock, turkeys and gobbler, ducks and drake, geese and gander, sheep and ram. And two very angry raccoons.

Mrs. Carpenter feeds about 25 racoons every night and Mr. Carpenter took time out that first night to capture two of them with a large fishnet. He wasn't sure if they were male and female—and they were far too furious to let him find out—but he hoped.

Mr. Carpenter was distressed that they couldn't save more of the wild things. He was damn sure Noah couldn't have done it either.

They talked about sand for the tunnel filters. Too dense. Layers of blankets. Not solid enough.

It was Mrs. Carpenter who thought of the popcorn. She might not have if it had not been a very sore subject indeed. Four hundred-pound sacks of unpopped popping corn is more popcorn than all the children on Madronna could ever eat, but that was what that idiot Elinor Filibruster had ordered for the school party. And without a word, mind, to Mrs. Carpenter.

The women got out their frying pans.

They have proper filters for the tunnel now, in case the world gets crazy again. But that first time they used feed sacks stuffed with popcorn.

IT was six a.m. when the phone rang. Lena Masterson reported from the lighthouse that old Robbie Robinson was coming round the point and he was flying the salmon flag.

Lena had dialed SOS so she had seven of us on the line. When Robbie flies the salmon flag that means he has more salmon than the island can possibly eat fresh. It means we will have to drop everything and can salmon. This early in July there should not be that many salmon running. This early in July it is extremely inconvenient to can salmon. Our first summer visitors have just arrived and need settling in. Trust old Robbie.

"Let's think a moment, girls," said Mrs. Carpenter. There was a pause cut by a sardonic eighth voice. "Why," asked old Les Chumley, who always listens in, especially when somebody else's number has been rung, "don't you take all your visitors to the community hall? Now you've stuck us with that expensive new stove it might as well be used." (The stove cost $50, was not new and both old Robbie and old Les voted against it. But it is certainly a fine big stove.)

"Splendid," said Mrs. Carpenter swiftly. "And Lester, start up your smokehouse. You can smoke the small fish for a picnic dinner."

"I'm cutting fire wood," complained Lester.

"You *were*," said Mrs. Carpenter. "Listen, girls, leave the guests to make their own breakfasts. Just bring bread and butter and garden greens. And your pressure cookers. Tell the guests they'll be picked up at three."

"I won't handle anything over four pounds," the complaining voice of Lester was saying as we all hung up.

Robbie guts and rough-scales his salmon while bringing them in, ever since we met him once and threw them all overboard because he hadn't. But they have to be thoroughly scaled.

Each cleaned salmon is then handed over to Mrs. Carpenter, who cuts them neatly, with a single blow of a cleaver, into lengths to fit a two-and-a-half-pound can. We pack them in the cans, adding to each a bit of the belly—which contains the oils—a teaspoon of sugar and a half teaspoon of salt. We set the cans in big baking dishes in the new stove's two ovens, close the doors on them for 15 minutes to sweat out any air, top up with more boiling water, seal their lids in place with Mrs. Carpenter's canning machine, and process them in our pressure cookers for four hours.

Fifty small salmon were smoking in Lester's smoke-house by the time we got the first batch of cans in the cookers. By 3 o'clock we had put down 120 cans of salmon, buttered 20 loaves of homebaked bread, mixed a washtub of greens with oil, vinegar and salt, not told old Robbie old Les was smoking his salmon (they don't speak and old Robbie would have been mad), permitted old Robbie to bring Pete the seal to take his choice of the salmon heads and tails, sent some island boats and some strange boats out to pick up guests (any boat that puts into Madronna on a salmon-canning day can expect chores) and welcomed 82 guests (the strangers stayed).

Old Lester moved among them passing out fishes. Mrs. Carpenter had made him wash his hands.

Unless you come some day to Madronna you will never taste real canned salmon (it has to be in the can no later than three hours after leaving the sea). And if old Lester is dead you will never taste real smoked salmon at all.

Our guests averaged two pounds of smoked salmon apiece.

W HAT you do to your hand?'' Mrs. Carpenter asked
Elwy Danson, pouring out his tea.

"Didn't," said Elwy, ladling in sugar with a bandaged
hand. "Shaughnessy bit me."

"Then I better call Doc Filbert to give you a tetanus
shot."

"No need," said Elwy. "He gave me a shot six months
ago. Last time Shaughnessy bit me."

"Why'd you let Shaughnessy bite you again? Miss that
look of his?''

"No. He'd been sitting on me an hour, cleaning himself
up after eating half a chicken. Then he turns his head and I
see the look, and I think, 'You SOB, this time I'll get you.'
And before I'm finished thinking he gets me by the thumb.
And off out the window like greased lightning. Clean
through to the bone," added Elwy, examining his bandaged hand with admiration.

"He likes a thumb," said Mr. Carpenter, contemplating
the base of his own left thumb. "But I tell you Elwy, you got
to be set for him the instant he gets on your knee.
Sometimes he'll lay there for an hour. Sometimes half a
minute. All you can be sure is, after he eats he'll hit. But he
always gives you that warning look ahead. Not much
ahead. But ahead."

"Who," asked Richard James, who was working with
the road crew that day because Elwy was letting him drive
the bulldozer, "is Shaughnessy?"

"Haven't you met him?" Mrs. Carpenter was surprised.
"But perhaps not. He wouldn't fancy swimming to your
houseboat. Shaughnessy is a 26-pound orange tomcat
who's gone wild. He calls on people for handouts. Then he
bites them."

"He never bites old Lester," said Mr. Carpenter, being fair.

"Lester raised him. Found him being stoned by a couple of summer kids," Mrs. Carpenter explained to Richard. "Just a kitten, he was. Lester clouted the kids and took Shaughnessy home. Patched him up and fed him by squeezing drops of milk into his mouth from his dishcloth. Of course Shaughnessy wouldn't bite Lester."

"You mean," said Richard, "that there's this big cat who goes around biting people, and *you let him*?"

"Well," said Mr. Carpenter defensively, "he's kind of a splendid cat, when he's not biting. Fur about two inches long. Got a black mask like a fox. Comes stalking in like he was people. And demands a handout. You couldn't hardly refuse. But he only bit me once. I get him first."

"How do you know he weighs 26 pounds?" asked Richard.

"Scooped him up from the back with a fishnet," said Mr. Carpenter. "And weighed the both of us. And then tossed Shaughnessy out the door (was he wild!) and weighed the fishnet and me. Difference was 26 pounds. Doc Filbert bet he wouldn't be more than 20, thought he was all fur."

"All tomcat," said Elwy. "Our cat's last litter is three orange with black masks. Fourth one's striped grey, like our tom. He lay up in the barn till Shaughnessy'd had his innings."

"Would he call on me," asked Richard, "if I left the gangplank down and a fish at the top?"

"Make it steak," said Elwy. "And watch for when he lays his ears flat and shoots you a sort of evil look."

"Getting to be too many orange cats," said Mrs. Carpenter. "Shaughnessy would be fine, if he was civilized. Next time he comes round here I'll bait the live trap and take him over to the vet on Cooper."

Sheer horror glared at her from three pairs of male eyes. "Elizabeth!" said Mr. Carpenter, his voice trembling with shock. "Don't you dare touch that cat!"

When they left Mrs. Carpenter watched them from the window. "They're taking the live trap," she said.

SUNDAY on Madronna is the day of rest after the Saturday night bath. Actually, in the summer time, shower. Or, if all the wells in your vicinity have gone dry, sponge.

Last Sunday Charlie Jo phoned at 7:30 and invited us for breakfast. He asked us to holler Richard James off his houseboat and bring him too. The Carpenters, he said, were on their way.

To get to the Jo boat we had to go half way round the island and into a little bay by Sunset Head. There isn't a road over the mountain so as well as hollering up Richard we hollered up a ride on his power boat. Too hot to walk, at least for our six summer visitors.

The bay where the Joes anchor their boat gets a lot of drift. So does the bay on the other side of Sunset Head. It's because they're off active water, with very little protection.

Charlie Jo caught our lines, helped us ashore and introduced our visitors to his grandmother and grandfather, mother and father, younger brother and sister and the two Brothers who are holidaying with them on their 30-foot boat.

"Now first," he said, "you've got to come and see your breakfast where Brother John found it." He led us down the beach. There, half buried in the sand just at high-tide mark, was a five-pound tin of canned ham. "Now, around the mountain," said Charlie, and we followed him along a deer trail over the spur of the mountain into the other bay. There, half buried in the sand just at high-tide mark, was a 10-pound tin of powdered eggs.

"I was afraid you'd think even Brother John was spinning tales if you didn't see it for yourself," explained Charlie. "It's a record," said Mr. Carpenter. "I thought

I'd seen everything that drifted in, including bod—'' ''Not before breakfast, James,'' said Mrs. Carpenter, "After?" asked one of my visiting professors, hopefully.

We had a nice peaceful breakfast round the campfire on the shore by the Jo boat. Mary Jo, Charlie's mother, had fresh salmon grilse for the visitors—she knew they'd be afraid of anything out of a can washed up by the sea. And the peace was not disturbed by a boat a quarter of a mile off shore that was plainly in need of rescue. "Been there since daybreak," said Joseph Jo. "Thought they were just fishing, but finally put the glasses on them and they're waving and yelling."

"Out of gas," said Mr. Carpenter sadly, "mainlanders." "And no lifejackets, no paddle, no flares, no flashlight even, I bet," said Joseph, "sixth in a week." "They'll be more educated after breakfast," said Charlie. But we kept an eye on them, in case they started swimming.

Sunday peace. Excellent ham. Splendid scrambled eggs. And over all the scent of the sea.

"Most nostalgic scent I know," said my other visiting professor, lying back in the sand and watching Grandma Jo knit an Indian sweater, carding the raw yarn with her teeth.

"Yeah," said Charlie. "Remember that time we smelled it, Brother Mark? The time you took our class on a tour to Ontario and Quebec to see our country, and the bus driver took us down by the Toronto beaches. And this smell comes in the windows and for a minute we're back on the islands. Not a dry eye in the bus."

"Until," said Brother Mark, "the bus driver explains it isn't the sea. It's the Ashbridge's Bay sewage treatment plant."

MILDRED Stonehenge is 92, survivor of an island pioneer family, as independent as they come, can still drop a deer with one shot from her rifle (in or out of season) and has a fine sense of humor; but there is no question that at times she can be an old curmudgeon.

At the moment she is carrying on a guerilla war against her tenant, Holly Jopdale, because Holly has declined a proposal of marriage by Mildred on behalf of Mildred's great-grandson John (who doesn't know anything about it) in favor of a proposal from Elwy Danson's brother Jason.

To be accurate, the war has been off and on ever since Holly rented the dining room and butler's pantry (kitchen and outhouse shared) in Mildred's elderly mansion on the hill. Mildred was born on the island to parents who came out from the old country in the 1860s and built accordingly.

Nobody knows how much money she has, but it's not much. Mr. Carpenter persuaded her to take the basic old-age pension, because everybody gets it. She will not, however, submit to any needs, means or other test to determine if she is entitled to other aid. But things must be a bit tight because she agreed, upon representation from Mrs. Carpenter, to take a roomer. Holly, who has a government grant to record on tape the reminiscences of the island's oldtimers, is the roomer.

Mildred accepted the roomer, but not that the roomer could shut her door. Whenever Holly had company, she could expect Mildred. If Mildred was pleased with Holly at the time, she would tap on the door, march in bearing a gift of cookies, look the guests over and say in a loud stage whisper "Get them out!" If Mildred was not pleased with Holly she would bring old Robbie Robinson with her, charge in without knocking, show Robbie through Holly's rooms—including Holly's cupboards and drawers—and announce to the assembled guests, "Mr. Robinson is moving in here as soon as I get rid of *her*."

Since the rejected marriage proposal Holly has put a lock on her door and Mildred and Robbie parade up and down the long verandah outside Holly's living-room, bending beady eyes upon the guests.

Holly used to get even by inviting her guests to take baths. Mildred has lots of water from an artesian well, unlike most of the islanders, but she is sure Holly will run it dry ("I listen to her running that water and the sweat stands out on my brow!"). She has removed the toilet which she says takes nine gallons to flush.

Holly and Jason (who is a fisherman) have every intention of living at Mildred's after their marriage, and Mildred has every intention that they shall; but there are scores to be kept. So the wedding shower we threw for Holly (Mildred declining to attend) was rather special. Mrs. Carpenter was doubtful at first, but finally agreed to go part way.

We were all set when the clump-clump of feet mounting Holly's steps was heard. As Mildred and Robbie marched along the verandah, they beheld a picture. Center, looking heavenward, was Mrs. Carpenter, wearing corsets, brassiere and bloomers. To right and left, also looking heavenward, was the rest of Madronna womanhood, wearing not a stitch.

Old Robbie, escaping, fell over the verandah rail. But Mildred was waiting for us when we left. "I'll be at your wedding," she told Holly, and then she bent a tart eye on Mrs. Carpenter. "You ought to take off some of that lard, Elizabeth," she said.

ONE of the advantages of living below the poverty line on Madronna is that you don't take the garden (or the fruit and nut trees) out of the backyard. And you look for wild food. You become a natural, not a cultivated, gourmet. The materials are at hand.

Fiddleheads can be frozen and shipped anywhere. But they might as well have stayed home. They have lost the flavor that gives them the right to aspire to a superior table. They are now gone till next spring, of course, and we are reduced to spinach and Swiss chard (mostly chard, the deer won't eat chard).

The broad beans are coming on early. With broad beans time from garden to table is of the absolute essence. Even a farmer's market gets them there too late. And green peas, out in the world, are the most debased of vegetables. They cannot possibly reach the market without becoming mere fodder.

The list is endless. Nobody has really tasted new baby carrots if they came to the pot more than two hours after pulling. Nobody has really tasted radishes who has not pulled *white* radishes minutes before lunch.

One advantage of being near the source of supply is that no gardener ever grows just enough for his own requirements. Sometimes it is not an advantage. Islanders have been known to hide in their woodsheds to evade old Les Chumley, bearing cabbages. It doesn't help. He goes in and leaves them on your kitchen table. You are then faced with either having chickens to feed them to (which is a problem unless you were prescient about Les and cabbages), or learning how to make sauerkraut, or wasting good food, which is not permissible.

With Mildred Stonehenge and her two walnut trees the

fee is different. Where Lester wants gratitude, Mildred wants walnuts. Her two trees were planted before she was, and at 92 she no longer cares to climb after her crop. Anybody else is welcome to climb and harvest, but the understanding is—one sack for Mildred, one sack for me.

The trees are very large and produce more walnuts than Madronna can eat. And a funny thing about them — although they were planted long before somebody was supposed to have developed soft-shell walnuts, they bear soft-shell walnuts. You can crack them with your hands. The better housekeepers always pickle some of them, but pickling walnuts is a chore and it gives you black hands which you then have to bleach, which splits your knuckles. It is easier to develop a distaste for pickled walnuts.

The better housekeepers also dry their walnuts in their attics. This keeps the house tidy but produces rubbery walnuts. The only way to dry walnuts is to hang them up in a sack behind a wood stove. And the only way to eat them is in a messy fashion, sitting at ease before a roaring winter fire, cracking them with your hands, throwing the shells into the fire, and missing.

That is also where you ought to eat your steamed butter clams. A bucket of clams to each guest, a toothpick to dig out the clams, a platter of drawn butter into which to dip them, and an old washtub to throw the shells at.

When I started this I meant to touch on other delicacies—salmon grilse (you can't buy them), oysters so big they slop over the edges of a bread-and-butter plate, home-smoked bacon, and mushrooms. But there isn't time. Except perhaps to warn Captain O'Grady that if he comes stealing mushrooms in my orchard next month there will be bear traps.

M UUH-MUUH!''

And wherever you are you rush madly down or up to the glassed-in kitchen porch, grabbing the broom. Because if you don't, the humming bird beating its tiny self against the glass will be a dead humming bird.

What you do is, you put the broom against the glass above the humming bird and press it gently but quickly down into your waiting free hand, and close your hand on it, and step to the door and open your hand. If you have not been quick enough the little weightless bundle of feathers will never rise again. But if you have, it will lie on your hand for a moment, and you will feel one of the tiniest hearts in the world beating against your fingers, and then it will take off like a bullet.

If, a minute later, you pass too near its nest, it will divebomb you.

No gratitude.

The panic of a humming bird in the porch is at odds with everything else about a humming bird. It seems to fear nothing but losing its freedom.

It must also be one of nature's most concentrated bits of malevolence. None of the casualties of the porch has ever weighed as much as half an ounce on Mrs. Carpenter's spice scale. But any of them will take on a blackbird, or even a crow. And one of the most prized pictures on the island is a snap Mr. Carpenter caught of four humming birds beating up Shaughnessy, the 26-pound orange tomcat who rules this end of the island.

Being mean to a cat, especially Shaughnessy, is nobility in a bird. But the humming birds are also vicious to each other.

There's a ruby-throat who seems to be in charge of our

point. To try to tempt the humming birds away from the quince and honeysuckle which attract them into the kitchen porch, we have hung nectar bottles from a clothes line on the front verandah. This ruby-throat sits on the very top of a deadspar pinetree outside. Just sits there. And not one of the 30 or so humming birds buzzing around dares go near the nectar bottles. If a new boy does, old Ruby-throat drills him like a pistol shot.

When he's good and ready, old Ruby-throat goes down and takes a sup from each of the six nectar bottles, and then retires to his deadspar. After that the other humming birds rush in, in an established order, and take their nectar. It's only the very young birds, at the tail end of the feed, who dare to dispute the seniority line, and then only with each other.

Since old Ruby likes to feed every 20 or 25 minutes, it doesn't leave a lot of time for anybody else.

Some of our more tidy neighbors have suggested that we ought to take that deadspar pinetree out. But we wouldn't dare. Old Rube would attend to the woodsman.

For a while there, we thought our humming birds were real gluttons, because every morning the nectar bottles were empty. But one night we got back late from the community hall and coming up from the float we heard a scuttle on the verandah. Stopping dead and waiting, we finally made out two raccoons, standing on the verandah railing and methodically swilling nectar. First one bottle and then the next.

So we moved the clothes line and the nectar bottles to the middle of the verandah, where there isn't a handy railing. Now the nectar would last five days, but we change it on the fourth day before it starts to ferment.

Ever been kept off your own front verandah by 30 drunk humming birds?

THE word swept through the island like a slash fire. Ed Foulkes had television.

Madronna has not remained free of television because of any higher sense of values, but because we can't get it. Various visiting experts said from the first we couldn't: too far from a transmitter, and in any case the mountains would block it. Some people bought sets anyway (second-hand, of course) and proved the experts right. Snow was what they got, just snow.

And then Ed Foulkes, working quietly away at the other end of the island, got a whole day's programs with hardly any snow at all.

"He figures," reported Mr. Carpenter, "that the image is bouncing off Porter Mountain, right on to his antenna. He's got one of those antennas you can turn around. He's been working it around a degree or two at a time, and I must say he's got a very good picture."

"Want to go and look?" asked Mrs. Carpenter.

Certainly I wanted to go and look. All the rest of the island had already looked and the children were up there right now. So I shoved a corned beef roast into the Dutch oven for the paying guests' dinner and accepted a ride in Irwin Hoffstater's taxi.

The Foulkes are a couple of indeterminate age who have a large garden, raise rabbits rather than hens and sell snowdrop bulbs and flowers to bring in some cash. They send the flowers to market in a big suitcase every boat day during the early spring season, and they get a good price. The snowdrops are bigger than anything on the mainland, about the size of a junior daffodil.

The proceeds have given them just enough to get by and pursue their ambition to be the first Madronna household to have television.

Esther greeted us at the back door. "Ed'll be so pleased you came," she said in a reverently muted voice—we could hear the television from the living room. "Maybe you'd have a cup of coffee first. We've blacked out all the windows in there. Of course Ed knows he shouldn't do that indefinitely, but while he's perfecting the image it helps to have the greatest possible contrast."

She poured out our coffee and moved back to the stove to put on another pan of popcorn. "The children are in there with Ed," she said. "They've been as good as gold. Of course, I suppose it seems like magic to them."

At this point the living-room door opened and Johnny Cuthbert appeared. "Mr. Foulkes would like some more popcorn and carrots," he said.

Esther supplied the necessities. Then she turned to us. "Would you like to look?" she asked.

We crept in behind Johnny. In the darkened room the children were lined up in rows, sitting on the floor either side of Ed Foulkes. They were eating popcorn, but their eyes were on the screen where there was, indeed, a nearly snow-free picture.

Ed was sitting in an arm chair, with a small table of refreshments at his elbow. From the kitchen door we got him in profile. His eyes were fixed on the screen. So were the eyes of the white rabbit sitting on his lap. The rabbit was wearing a diaper. As we watched, Ed reached out, without ever removing his eyes from the screen, and put a carrot between the rabbit's front paws. Then he reached out again and found a handful of popcorn. He and the rabbit munched in unison. Their eyes never left the screen.

We'll have to go back another day to watch television.

IT was the summer visitors who brought garage sales to Madronna. The islanders had never thought of selling their rubbish.

But after two visiting families had put on a garage sale, Mildred Stonehenge decided to try her luck. Mildred, we think but cannot prove, is getting very hard up. She is 92 and lives in a huge old house which was built in the 18-somethings and furnished from England; and she has her pride.

The island folk-rock band offered to set up the sale, and she posted notices in the store and on the wharf.

Except for the band and us other helpers, two batches of summer visitors got there first. Three strangers—two men and a woman—poked around for about five minutes and said they'd take the chaise longue, which Mildred had priced at $5. They had paid the $5 and were setting the chaise longue in the sold area, when the second batch of visitors arrived. Among them was my visiting professor of history.

After glancing in horror at some of the prices he came running up to Mildred. "No, no, Mrs. Stonehenge," he cried, "you are charging far too little." He looked wildly around at a spinning wheel, $2, a barrel churn, $1, an old copper boiler, 50 cents. "How much did you get for that chaise longue?" he asked. "Five dollars," said Mildred.

"Then you must return it," said the historian to the two men who were putting it in the sold area. "It is worth at least $800. It would be immoral."

"We paid the price asked," one of the men retorted. "They paid the price asked," agreed Mildred tonelessly.

"This is most distressing," cried the historian. "But Mrs. Stonehenge, I must insist that you cancel the rest of the sale." The two men and the woman picked up the chaise longue and started down the hill. "If you wish to sell these things I will put you in touch with a reputable antique house."

"But I've already offered them for sale," said Mildred.

Charlie Jo, the leader of the rock-folk band, snatched the five-dollar bill from her hand, jerked his head at the band, and started after the chaise longue movers.

"Then I cancel the sale," declared the historian. "Didn't you know?" he appealed to the rest of us. But no, we hadn't known. We can be pretty dumb about the finer things in life.

We were putting the sale back in Mildred's house when the folk-rock band returned, bearing the chaise longue. "We Death-Walked them," said Charlie Jo with satisfaction.

"You *what*?" gasped the historian.

"Like this," said Charlie. The band snapped into line. Its five faces went blank, its five pairs of arms folded. It walked slowly, its five blank faces turned to an imaginary chaise longue moving crew. "Inside," explained Charlie, "we're thinking them small, smaller. They're beginning to shimmer as if they were walking in heat. They're getting smaller. They're getting dimmer. By the next bend, or the next bend, they'll fade from sight. No word said. No hand laid on.

"Works great with kids at a rock concert," he explained, relaxing. "Worked great with that bunch too. After they dropped the chaise longue I had to put the five-dollar bill in the woman's purse. They didn't any of them have the strength to hold it."

"Witchcraft!" cried the delighted historian. "Young man, would you please sit down and tell me, at rather greater length ..."

They sat on the chaise longue and we carried the rest of the sale around them, back into Mildred's house.

LES Chumley told us that the Robertsons were putting in the first plate glass window ever on Madronna Island. He knew because he had listened to Thorn Robertson ordering the glass on the party line. He told us how big the plate glass was going to be—six feet by seven—and how much it would cost and what the sales tax would be and when it would arrive on the SS Lady Lucinda.

Listening in on the party line is considered a social sin by those islanders who do not listen in. This does not, however, prevent them from listening to what others have heard. So we all know about the Robertsons' plate glass window.

Just like we all knew when the millionaire who owned Lily Island sold it. We knew that because he had phoned the caretaker to tell him. What we do not know is who has bought it.

Lily Island, which is just its local not its map name, is about 160 acres. In the spring it has lilies all over it which are not, according to one of our visiting botanists, lilies at all. But lilies will do for us. Lily Island is only about a quarter of a mile away from Madronna, although it is divided from us by a strong tidal current which can be tough to battle in a storm. In spite of that it is a kind of cousin to Madronna, and we naturally want to know who has bought it and what is going to be done with it next.

The other islanders think they know but they don't. They think they know because Mrs. Carpenter phoned me and we had a prearranged conversation. Mrs. Carpenter told me that the federal Government had bought it for a penitentiary. I asked her what kind of a penitentiary, and she said, "Maximum security, whatever that means."

Mr. Carpenter, who is not in Mrs. Carpenter's confidence in the matter of penitentiaries, is quite distressed. He thinks there could be escapees, in spite of that tidal current, and of course they would come to Madronna, and of course we couldn't turn them over to the law. You can't do that with hunted men. Perhaps they could work in Thorn Robertson's sawmill.

Elinor Filibruster is getting up a petition to send to the federal Government to say that Madronna will positively not accept a penitentiary on Lily Island. Elwy Danson is getting up a counter-petition (he always counters when Elinor petitions) to invite the penitentiary to Lily Island. He says it would be good for the logging, milling and fishing business, and is getting rather more signatures than Elinor.

Mrs. Carpenter and I have signed both petitions. Mildred Stonehenge has signed neither. She says she has had two relatives who have done time and she couldn't see that they were any worse than the rest of the clan. But she has been oiling up her rifle collection.

In the meantime Mrs. Carpenter and I have decided to visit the Thorn Robertsons and see their plate glass window. We know that it arrived on Saturday, because we saw the right-sized box marked fragile come off the Lady Lucinda. And we know Thorn put it in yesterday, because he phoned for Irwin to take over a lot of that tarry string stuff they use for packing windows; and it was six hours before Irwin got back. So that means Irwin helped him.

But we don't know anything officially.

We will just drop in for a cup of tea.

The rest of the island will be dropping in, too.

We can discuss what we're going to do with all those convicts.

THE gale warnings were out but no thunderbolt had actually been hurled when the regional road foreman, on the telephone to Madronna Island's road foreman, said the words, "And we'll want you to put a trail up to the Brown property." At which point the first thunderbolt *was* hurled, the telephone went dead, and Madronna was presented with an opportunity the regional road foreman ought to have known we couldn't resist.

Madronna's roads are intermittent. We have one going up and over the mountains and curling down into June Harbor. We have another running for six miles along the Channel side. They are not connected, though divided by only half a mile, because it would cost quite a bit to blast that half-mile road up the mountain and the politicians have never figured that we had enough votes to justify it. The community is thus cut in half.

But now our road forman, Jim Carpenter, had been given an order. A trail to the Brown property. What the district foreman overlooked is that we have two Brown properties. One was very recently acquired by a political Brown. The other, at the top of The Gap, has always been known as the Brown Property.

It must have been meant. Because the compressor was on the island for its one week in each year. You need a compressor if you are going to drill holes in a mountain to set off dynamite to carve out a road bed.

With the phones out the crew had to be collected in person. Elwy Danson's bulldozer was on this side, so Charlie Jo was sent round by boat to wheedle his retired bulldozer out of Jarge Gallagher. Jarge objects to his pensioners working, but he does live on the other side of The Gap. He agreed to start at the top end, where the

105

bulldozer could make some distance because it wasn't solid rock. The Government-grant crew, augmented by the younger able-bodied females, went into the middle stretch, with shovels, to clear surface soil away for the compressor.

Mr. Carpenter was the powder man, with Captain O'Grady for his monkey.

They drilled, packed, hollered fire till the hollering had been echoed by all of us up the mountain and everybody had taken shelter, blasted, and Elwy moved in with his bulldozer to clear. And then back to drilling, packing, hollering, blasting and clearing. While Jarge worked at the top and the rest of us worked in the middle. And one team was sent out to drop enough trees on the telephone line to keep the regional foreman out of communication. And another to place Dan Potter under house arrest with Mrs. Carpenter. Dan Potter has moral objections to dynamite. Also, his house is just below. He only got two rocks through his roof.

Busiest three days I ever remember.

But when the SS Lady Lucinda came round the point, bearing the regional foreman, Elwy and Jarge and their bulldozers were pushing the last of the rock from The Gap.

Mrs. Carpenter drove the regional foreman over the new road—bumpety bump—to where the work crew stood in tired glory. She drove him in the fire truck, which the men have not allowed the women to play with. She was followed by Mildred Stonehenge in the pumper, which the men have not allowed the women to play with. The men being out of the way, they had spent the last three days practicing.

Mrs. Carpenter ignored the universal male scowl. She jerked her head at the regional foreman.

"He says you built the wrong road," she told us.

NOW if Mrs. Carpenter were in charge, the islanders would simply build a house on the Madronna Indian Reserve for the Jo family.

The house is needed because Grandma Jo is having trouble with her arthritis, and the 30-foot Jo boat is crowded with Grandma and Grandpa Jo, Joseph and Mary Jo, Charlie, Augustine and Elizabeth Jo, and sundry visitors (at present two Brothers from Charlie's old school, but always somebody). Also, the boat is cold in winter.

But Mrs. Carpenter is not in charge.

After she noted, at a Sunday morning breakfast on the shore by the Jo boat, that Grandma Jo's hands were so crippled she could knit only very slowly, she Took Things Up. This entailed calling Doc Filbert, who agreed that Grandma needed a dry-land home, and consulted with the men of the family, Grandpa, Joseph and Charlie, all of whom agreed that it would be a good idea if Grandma had a dry-land home. They even went up with Mrs. Carpenter and Grandma and selected exactly the right spot for the house—above the bay where the Joes anchor their boat and with Sunset Head to break the high winds.

After that, however, the action slowed to that of a caterpillar who has an entire tree to consume all by himself.

First, the whole Jo family had to talk it over and decide, not by majority vote but by consensus, whether they wanted to stay at Madronna or go to the reserve on another island from which they had come and where there were lots of houses that would be glad to receive them. As Mrs. Carpenter said, this meant that even Augustine and Elizabeth, who would be going away to school in the winter anyway, could have a veto. "Of course!" said Grandma Jo and Mr. Carpenter in unison. "It's their home too."

So the subject was considered. And considered and considered. And considered. After which Grandpa Jo explained to the rest of us that the Joes had decided to stay on Madronna. Or rather—as Mrs. Carpenter showed signs of ordering up work parties—*by* Madronna. Because, equally of course, the chief and the council of the band that owned the Madronna Reserve and to which the Joes belong would have to decide—again by consensus—whether it would be a good thing to build a house on the Madronna Reserve. It has no houses now.

So at the moment Grandma Jo and Augustine and Elizabeth Jo have moved in with Mrs. Carpenter, and Mr. Carpenter and Grandpa Jo and Joseph Jo and Charlie Jo (with Mary Jo and the Brothers to cook and advise) have gone to the other reserve to consult with the chief of the council. At least the chief, and probably the chief and the council, will return with Grandpa and Joseph and Charlie to consider the subject on the spot.

In the meantime Mrs. Carpenter is fuming and Grandma Jo is knitting Mr. Carpenter an Indian sweater. She is making it from raw wool, carding it with her teeth as she works, and it will be a perfect sweater for fishing, elegant with an eagle in vegetable dye and absolutely windproof. As Mrs. Carpenter says, in a store it would cost more than $100.

Mrs. Carpenter thinks Grandma should make these valuable sweaters to sell in a store. But Grandma, gently, says no.

"In stores," says Grandma, "they want things on time. Their time."

ROUND this time of a summer the islanders' patience with mainland incompetence begins to wear thin. It never wears out entirely, not necessarily because compassion flourishes any more vigorously on Madronna than anywhere else but because, as Charlie Jo put it (going out to rescue the third boat in a week that had tangled with a sub-surface reef plainly marked on all the charts), "we need their inferiority to prove our superiority."

I guess you could say that by this time of the summer we are collecting special cases. Like the young couple in the power boat who ran out of gas on the Channel side just as darkness was falling. They were carried by the tide—not having oars or a paddle—to a beach which is not more than 300 yards from at least four houses. They had no flares and no flashlight; maybe the trees hid the house lights. Instead of camping in their beached boat for the night, they set out to find civilization. They stumbled up and down our two major mountain ranges, crossed two roads and fell into the Robertsons' kitchen for breakfast.

They walked clean across the island, at least four and a half miles, much of it straight up or straight down, with no light but the stars and the thinnest of moons. They passed within shouting distance of half the islanders. In fact, it remains a matter for marvel how they failed to run into any of us—it is Mr. Carpenter's theory that actually they walked about eight miles, accidentally skirting us.

But the really special thing about them, Thorn Robertson told us, was that scratched and tattered as they were, they were still cheerful. It made it possible for him to be genuinely kindly about getting out his boat and going round the island to gas up *their* boat...which they had **neglected** to tie to anything and was now half-way across the Channel on the early tide.

Mr. Carpenter is the only resident who never gets fed up with mainlanders, but then, he hardly ever gets fed up with anybody. He did take Colin Lose out of the last Christmas tree party and knock him out, but that was because Colin was making the kind of remarks about Santa Claus that might have disturbed the childrens' faith.

But by and large he holds to the belief that even the most regrettable types have something to contribute. Even the man who took his two young sons fishing and ran out of gas just beyond the lighthouse. They had nothing to signal with, just enough water and food to run out after the first half-day, no fishing gear and—of course—no means of getting to shore. The tide and the currents took them, over the next three days, in and out of sight of the lighthouse at widely spaced intervals, as though they were summer regulars fishing. It was only when Lena Masterson began to wonder why the same boat kept appearing each ebb tide that she put the glasses on them and they were brought in.

"Sure he should have been more careful," said Mr. Carpenter. "But I forgot how terrible the sea can be till I saw that man's eyes. I'll remember again now, for a while."

He pondered the other terrible things he had seen nature do to people, and not always careless people. "We got to stick together," he said.

And then he added, "I never put but one person off this island, and I regret that one. He was a murderer and he blew his nose on the post office floor, but he could set a saw better than any man I ever knew."

MADRONNA'S folk-rock band is beginning to be noticeable, but it all happened rather accidentally.

Mrs. Carpenter made their costumes, and all she had to work with at the time was a bolt of black sateen that she got at the garage sale of the undertaker on Cooper Island. So when they are doing folk they look like scarecrows. And when they are doing rock they look like witches and warlocks.

They got the three-wheeled plastic pedal-car after an anti-pollutionist brought it to Madronna and then kicked it off the government wharf. There is no blacktop on our roads, and the car's tires are pretty wide—almost as wide as a small automobile's—for turning by leg power. An afternoon's peddling convinced the anti-pollutionist that Madronna was 90 per cent upgrade.

When the band fished the car out of the drink he said they could have it.

It catches attention. It is cast out of plastic, light enough to be tipped up with one hand and shallow enough to be stored in a clothes closet (or the back of a boat). Two of the band, taking turns, sit in its two bucket seats and pedal, two others sit crosslegged in the space behind and the fifth—leader Charlie Jo when they're making an appearance—sits on the back.

They have made up to 45 miles an hour going down a hill in a mainland city, but their usual pace is about 15 miles an hour. Since there are so few of these vehicles, nobody has got around to barring them from the highway. This one, tooling along at 15 miles an hour, may some day trigger a real motorist into manslaughter.

They inherited The Macaw from Mr. Carpenter one week after he brought it home from a pet shop. Mrs.

Carpenter will not put up with profanity.

The Macaw likes to ride on the windshield of the pedal-car, flapping its wings to keep its balance and hurling raucous shrieks at passers-by. It will also ride on Charlie's left shoulder, but when it goes into a building—say a hotel or an arena—it prefers to walk. People always make way for it. Probably that beak, although it is an amiable bird. It walks into a concert ahead of the band, and then takes its place on Charlie's shoulder.

About the band's rock sound I am not qualified to comment. A critic on the mainland described it enthusiastically as "new." That was accurate. The band's instruments are all created (one of each only) by a recluse who lives on top of Porter Mountain and scratches a living by making recorders. To my ear they sound as though they all wail in different keys, like assorted souls specially delivered from hell. When they are all going—and The Macaw—it is noisy.

The band treats its fans rough. That is only proper coming from a plastic pedal-car full of witches and warlocks. For one thing, when Charlie claps his left hand around The Macaw's beak and brings his instrument up to his chest that means, "You out there, shut up. Or we walk out." And if the fans don't shut up, the band does walk out. Usually, they have planned to go to the canoe races anyway.

But more and more they get a breathless stillness. It has an effect. The gaudy bird, and the black, forbidding five, evil-wishing their audience. But the other evening The Macaw rather spoiled the deadly atmosphere. When Charlie uncorked him after the pandemonium had hushed, he turned his head and remarked cheerfully into the silence: "Noisy bunch of buggers, aren't they?"

I THINK somebody once wrote a sonnet to strawberries but I can't make Bartlett's prove it and in any case on Madronna it would have been to blackberries.

Blackberries are distinctive, delicious and go on forever. That is, from the last week in July to the first frost. They are also almost everywhere. People who prefer solitude have their own secret patches, and people who prefer company congregate at the big patch at the bottom of old Les Chumley's (Cholmondeley's) place. Les loves to be hospitable and it is one of the few things he has to be hospitable with.

Blackberries are made into pies, preserves, jam, jelly and wine. And vinegar, which is not intended but happens when a careless wine-maker neglects to bottle her wine early enough, after which I *call* it vinegar and make purple salads.

Picking blackberries takes thousands of hours of the islanders' time. It requires an awful lot of blackberries to make the 150 gallons of wine that old Les puts down every year, and the 100 gallons that Mrs. Carpenter does, and they are only the big producers.

Summer visitors can usually be drafted into picking blackberries (you always give them a jar of blackberry jam or a bottle of blackberry vinegar to take home). And the children will do it for short periods on a one-fer basis (one-fer-me and one-fer-mum).

Old Les does it on an assembly-line basis. He slings gallon-buckets on a rope around his waist and when one is full he pulls an empty into place. He is a moving collector's item of old gallon buckets, peanut butter, golden syrup, molasses, honey, lard, maple syrup. Maple syrup really did once come in gallon buckets—the evidence is there every summer, hanging on Les's stomach. Time was, too, when he could fill all his buckets in three hours, but the years have climbed aboard his ancient frame and knotted his old hands.

While we pick at his patch we also gossip. Yesterday Lettie Danson warned us that when we go for cards to her place tomorrow night she will be using Elwy's oldest greasiest packs and would we please bring ours. "Somebody," she said, "has to show Elinor Filibruster."

We knew what she meant. Elinor is always trying to improve our standards of behavior. Last card night was at her place, and at each table she had two brand new unbroken packs of cards. The room was elegantly lighted with candles. "We'll be using the barn lanterns," explained Lettie.

"Do you remember the time just after we came here," said Helen Jessup, "when Elinor told me it wasn't correct—oh, pardon me, Les (as she banged into him from behind)—to wear lisle hose to the Community Hall?"

"And we all had to wear lisle hose for months," said Mrs. Carpenter, banging into Les in her turn. "Of course we had to put Elinor in her place, but lisle hose are far too durable, Helen. I've still got mine, and they always did wrinkle around the ankles."

"We could dye them green and red to fill them for the children at the Christmas tree," said Lettie. "Oh, excuse me, Les," as her bucket clashed with a bucket on the collector's rump.

Old Les is always surprised at how quickly his buckets come up full. But not very surprised. "Told you the old man could still beat you all at picking blackberries," he chortles at us, and goes bucketing home. Peanut butter, golden syrup, molasses, honey, lard and maple syrup.

ON Madronna Island the air is so clear you can read by moonlight. I tell you this of my own knowledge.

The other night I wakened to a call of nature and considered the matter. Owing to the curious construction of our house it would be necessary, to reach the bathroom, to go through the adjoining bedroom, where four summer visitors were sleeping, through the hall, where two summer visitors were bedded down in sleeping bags, and through the kitchen, where other sleeping bags were laid out and one visitor, who is scared of mice, was sleeping on the table. So I decided to hop out the window.

The window opens outward on a rod with a knob at the end of it, and as I hopped I hung up. My nightgown snagged on the knob and hiked up to my armpits and left me swinging there, facing out into a night full of stars and the moon.

I tried to shake loose, but the nylon in nightgowns is strong. I tried to reach the ground with my toes, but they couldn't make it. I tried walking back up the wall, but that just gave me slivers in my feet, also my bottom. All exterior lumber on island houses is rough, owing to the island mill not having a planer. I tried reaching behind me to pull the nylon over the knob, but I couldn't get the necessary purchase.

I flapped my hand along the windowsill behind to see if it held anything that could puncture the nylon, and came up with a newspaper.

So there I hung, naked to the armpits, and read that a city council somewhere had voted 12 to three against installing a secondary sewage treatment plant.

It made a delicate situation.

One good yell would, of course, bring all kinds of

assistants. To be exact, 22 of them—they were up for the weekend barbecue. (I could only be sure that my own family would sleep soundly through the uproar.) But how would summer visitors judge the competence of a guest-house operator whom they had to rescue from such a predicament?

On the other hand, if I did not yell it would almost certainly be Captain O'Grady who discovered me. He and I are in a running battle over who shall enjoy the mushrooms in my orchard. They break earth during the night and I have found that if I do not get out there promptly the Captain will have them. So I have been getting out earlier and earlier, and so has the Captain.

We are now backed up to about five-thirty a.m.

I did not want the Captain to discover me. He would undoubtedly be a gentleman, shielding the lady with his shirt while he unhooked her, but it would put him ahead in the matter of mushrooms.

Eventually I got a fingernail through the nylon and started a rip that dropped me to earth, and the next day I went to the Carpenter's store and got six enamel chamberpots to put under the beds in our six bedrooms.

But on Madronna you can read by moonlight. If you can't think of anything else to do.

116

WHAT mainlanders call self-serve stores strike Madronna islanders as quaint. A mere beginning.

Most islanders collect their groceries on Saturday. That is the weekly boat day, so they can combine meeting the boat with taking in their mail, collecting their mail, doing the shopping and meeting their neighbors.

As Jim Carpenter is the postmaster as well as the storekeeper, he must put aside storekeeping to accept and process outgoing mail and sort and hand out incoming mail. Mrs. Carpenter has little time for the store on Saturdays, either, because she is receiving the islanders in the big kitchen in behind. Since almost everybody on the island (except the sick and recluses) arrives before the boat and does not leave until the mail is sorted, there are quite a few people to be received over a period of about three hours.

This means the store on its biggest day is empty of anything but customers.

Each family has its own account book, with the family name printed by Mr. Carpenter across the binding. As we collect our purchases we enter them in the book. If we know the price we enter that too, if not we leave it for Mr. Carpenter to do later.

It is quite an animated scene. Elinor Filibruster slices her bacon before anybody else because she slices it thinner than anybody else and she says it won't slice really thin if there is already grease on the blade. Elinor gets more breakfasts out of a pound of bacon than anybody else on Madronna. While somebody else is resetting the machine for a more generous slice, Elinor says to Richard James, "Will you kindly reach me down that bucket. Not THAT one, can't you see it's dinted? The next one."

She has interrupted Richard as he is making out the bill for an old-age pensioner who cannot read or write. We all know he can't, but only Mr. and Mrs. Carpenter and Richard *officially* know it. Probably, come to think of it, Elinor does not know. Who would tell her?

Colin Close is showing off his dog by having him fetch, on command, canned tomatoes, pork and beans and dog food. A stranger has come in off a boat and 12-year-old Johnny Cuthbert is ringing up his purchases on the cash register. "How much are four-inch nails the pound?" he hollers over the post office partition to Mr. Carpenter who hollers back and Johnny makes change. The Biggest Squirrel in These Parts has come into the store, as usual, and been given three peanuts. He is clutching two of them with his front paws, like an awkward father holding new twins, and standing over the third. Two younger squirrels are waiting, also as usual, for him to do what he must—abandon two of the peanuts and cart the third off for storage. Thorn Robertson and Elwy Danson are betting on how long it will take him to decide.

Captain O'Grady is stealing a pack of snuff. Just as he reaches the door, Mrs. Carpenter's hand closes on the back of his neck. (She is not always in the kitchen.) She seats herself on a nail keg, lays the scrawny little captain across her knee, and paddles him soundly on the bottom. "Now," she says, jerking him upright, "enter that snuff in your book. And you two," she says to Thorn and Elwy, "stop teasing those squirrels. Give the little chaps some peanuts too."

The Biggest Squirrel has outsmarted both his fellows and the gamblers. He is eating his three peanuts on the spot.

NOTHING ever works out the way you thought it would. After my visiting professor of history, during a garage sale at Mildred Stonehenge's, discovered that her big old house was stuffed with fine old antiques and stopped the sale, we thought her problems were solved. Mildred is 92 and she has her pride, so the $20 extra which the Government says it is going to give to old-age pensioners on the supplement would not help her, because she will not submit to the indignity of applying for the supplement. But, we told each other, she could sell the antiques one by one for proper prices, and that would see her through.

The historian prevailed upon a reputable antique house on the mainland to send up one of its experts to look the situation over.

The expert is a big, cadaverous chap who answers to the name of Sydney Hollows, ducking his head and gnawing on his knuckles while he does it. Shy. Perishing scared of Mildred, who is a tartar, until he lost all sight of her in the sight of all those beautiful antiques. (The rest of us had missed the beauty and still do.)

Holly Jopdale, who rents rooms from Mildred, reports that although she had her ear to the kitchen door, she could hear only some of Mildred's barks and Sydney's mumbles during the conversation which followed the tour of the house, but the gist was this:

Sydney likes the antiques—where they are. Mildred, now that she knows other people envy her possession of them, likes the antiques—where they are. Sydney is going to live in the attic and turn the barn into a workshop and restore the antiques.

"And," said Mildred, barging into the conference in the Carpenters' kitchen as Holly reached this point, "I shall

119

leave the house and its contents to the Madronna Community Club as a museum. Bearing my name. After I'm gone, of course. You will kindly remember in future, young woman," she told Holly balefully, "that you are living in a museum." (Holly is going to marry Jason Danson, who is a fisherman, and they are going to live at Mildred's, and they will be very kind to her when she needs it, but any place where they live will not look like a museum. There are going to be some dandy fights which both sides—and all the rest of us—will thoroughly enjoy.)

Meanwhile, there's the matter of money. How are Mildred and Sydney going to live on what wouldn't support Mildred, which was why she was selling the antiques in the first place? And what would Madronna do with a museum ("There'll be my collection of driftwood too," Mildred has pointed out) when there's no money to maintain it? What would Madronna do with a museum anyway? And somebody had better shut up old Les Chumley before he enlarges the project with his collection of old bottles and old gallon buckets.

Mr. Carpenter has phoned the historian who is going to lean on the antique house to pay Sydney to do his restoring of furniture on Madronna. Sydney has already sneaked back to the mainland and borrowed the antique house's $2,000 heavy-duty sewing machine; we are hoping RCMP Sergeant Munro will not be asked to consider it stealing. And Sydney, under the coaching of Mrs. Carpenter, is giving us lessons in upholstering. Ten dollars per student for the course.

We really wouldn't mind—most of our furniture could do with reupholstering—but Sydney is making us do it **RIGHT**.

120

THE grouse had her nest just past the Community Hall. We met her mate last May when we were taking Grandpa Cuthbert through the island to his rest in Madronna's graveyard. His coffin was on the back of the black-draped government truck, with Mr. Carpenter at the wheel. His eldest son was sitting beside Mr. Carpenter. The island's three other vehicles were carrying the old and the frail. The rest of us were walking behind. And then, on the narrow mountain road, the male grouse challenged Grandpa's passing.

He strutted back and forth across the road, back and forth, his stern little eyes shouting at us, "You'll get *them* only over my dead body."

So Grandpa's son got down from the truck and walked him off the road, taking a bit of a beating about the head while he did it—he had a black eye next day. But Grandpa had always asked the wild things, nicely, for passage.

The children found the nest, of course, getting their own thumping from grouse wings. They just looked, they didn't touch. Fourteen eggs.

But the second time back only 12, and one dead crow. The grouse had done their best, but there are more crows and they are organized.

We often say there are no predators on Madronna Island. What we mean is that there is nothing big enough to threaten us, or the deer. The smaller creatures have enemies.

When the mother grouse brought her nestlings out there were nine of them. Perhaps a coon had got the other three. Not a mink. A mink would have killed the whole lot after killing the parents, and eaten one. A rat might have sneaked in and stolen a single egg.

They stayed around the road above the Community Hall. When anybody passed the mother would give a chirrup of warning and the chicks would scuttle to the side of the road and freeze. At first they looked like little chips of wood, and then like little rounds of wood. Perfectly motionless. It got so that when the government truck passed, or any of the other three vehicles, or a bulldozer, they would move very slowly at the grouse place, sometimes stopping, while mum chirruped a tardy chick to the way side. She never hid herself, just stood as tall and visible as she could, well away from the chicks as if to say, "If it's grouse you want for dinner, look this way."

By the time they were learning to fly the hawks and the owls had been around too, and there were only five of them left. They seem to have a certain trust now in humans; they will practice their flying in front of us. They do not know that the hunting season is coming.

The children have plastered the road with No Hunting signs. They want to protect *their* grouse because they have seen that their grouse love enough to offer their lives for their children. But they will have good appetites for other grouse brought trussed and stuffed and glazed to table. They won't recognize them, you see, as the meat and bones of family affection.

We never do, we predators. Crow and coon and mink, rat and hawk and owl. And human.

B LACK widow spiders have been always with us, but it wasn't until one of them bit Elwy Danson that anybody on Madronna put a mind to the subject.

Elwy met his black widow in the old cedar log cabin on the mountain above Mildred Stonehenge's place. We are making the cabin habitable for Sydney Hollows, the antique-upholstery man, because it is obvious that if he can't get away from us for large parts of every day (and perhaps especially from Mildred), he will flee the island. He is a thin, shy, reclusive person, somewhere between 30 and 50, and he really can't stand large doses of people.

The cabin is maybe 100 years old, but being of cedar it has lasted, and after looking it over Mr. Carpenter declared it structurally sound. Neither Mr. Carpenter nor Sydney found anything objectionable in the fact that it had a dirt floor, but Mrs. Carpenter did. So that was what brought Elwy over the mountain on his bulldozer with a load of rough lumber on the skidder behind it. That was about five in the morning.

A couple of minutes later, as he stepped through the door, something fell on the back of his neck and he brushed at it and it bit him. Being experienced, up to a point, he ascertained what had done the biting, found it was what he thought was a black widow (red hourglass on bottom of abdomen), put it in an old bottle and got on with laying stringers for the floor. That was a mistake.

By the time Richard James and 12-year-old Johnny Cuthbert arrived about noon to help him Elwy was finding that wise men—even when they are six-four, young and brawny—don't always try to stick it out. He was on the dirt floor in terrible pain and beginning to arch on his heels and head.

They got him onto the skidder—four logs chained together—and roped him face down. If he had to arch they didn't want him breaking his back. Johnny got under the rope beside him with his arms around Elwy's head and shoulders so that when he came out of an arch he wouldn't smash his face, and Richard climbed into the bulldozer seat.

Richard, who is a writer, has been allowed to play with the bulldozer. "Zig-zag!" gasped Elwy, using his second word since their arrival, his first being "Widow!" with a jerk at his bottled attacker.

So they zig-zagged down the mountain, with trees crashing round them, the logs of the skidder lurching, heaving, sliding, the driver praying at the top of his lungs and six-foot-four of agony arching till its head nearly touched its heels. As Elwy said just yesterday, "If you'd arrived a bit later, you could have rolled me down the mountain like a hoop."

While they were administering antivenom in the mainland hospital to which he was flown they told him black widows hardly ever kill people, just their mates. But Richard has decided to determine the extent of the problem. He has phoned for our visiting entomologist, and led the children forth, in sou'westers and with jam jars baited with fruit flies, to collect specimens. Julie Bates found 27 in their barn. Johnny Cuthbert, who is dandy in a pinch but lacks the scientific approach, turned up with a single substantial sample.

"I had 11," he explained to Richard. "But I forgot to put in any flies. So the feed situation bein' what it was, they got down to one."

T HE trouble is," said Mrs. Carpenter, "that Mr. Carpenter hasn't seen the bishop. If he saw what a sad little bundle of bombast he is, he'd have to forgive him.

There is much about the bishop that requires forgiveness. He made Madronna the object of missionary charity, by persuading a Toronto parish to give us a church (without our knowledge or consent) when we were fixing up our own. He comes over from Cooper Island (a sin in itself) to lay down the spiritual law (to the seven people who turn up in the church and won't accept it anyhow). And he is the chief obstacle in the way of a marriage between Holly Jopdale and Jason Danson. She says she will be married only in the church; she has not actually been attending church. He says the only place he will not be married is the church.

"Although, mind you," said Mildred Stonehenge, "that's just the excuse. They've both developed the usual cold feet. I don't know if you know it (we do) but they've been shacked up together the last two months at my place. They're just shying at the contract."

"It's all excuses," said Mrs. Carpenter crossly. "Jed Peterson is mad because the bishop won't use the pulpit he built. Most of the island doesn't want to waste Sunday afternoons in a church anyway. I boil up myself everytime I look at the kneelers those Toronto characters covered with hand-made needlepoint. It might be bearable if all they'd given was money. We're all furious because Elinor Filibruster volunteered to be church secretary and the bishop let her. And Richard James and Charlie Jo and Mr. Carpenter are claiming smugly they've always said they weren't Christians—and just see how right they were!"

"Mr. Carpenter will be surprised to find himself in

heaven," agreed Mildred. "But he'll recover fast. In seconds he'll be arguing with the Lord to let the sinners in."

"The point is," said Mrs. Carpenter pointedly, "that the bishop and his church have split the island. The place is just seething with feuds. We've got to figure out a way to mend things."

It was a meeting of five of the seven who attend the bishop's church. We had not invited Elinor Filibruster, which meant that her poor little husband, whom the bishop had made warden, couldn't come either.

"What we need," said Mildred, who has made war every day of her 92 years, "is war. We've got to ginger the island into making the church over in its own image. Get them to tear out the bishop's pulpit and put in Jed's. Rip those awful shingles off the roof and put on cedar shakes. Auction those kneelers for fireside benches."

"And how," demanded Mrs. Carpenter, "do we get the islanders in the mood for war?"

"I'll tell you at the Community Club meeting for tomorrow night we're going to start calling now," said Mildred. "Thieving bunch, those Cooper islanders," she added. And then, more thoughtfully, "I daresay once he's met him, Mr. Carpenter won't mind putting in a word with the Lord for the bishop. I wouldn't mind if he did. I could even put up with Captain O'Grady in heaven, thief though he is. But are we going to have to endure an eternity of Elinor Filibruster?"

MADRONNA Island has captured its church from the bishop.

It began last night at a full meeting of the Community Club. Mrs. Carpenter took the podium first to remind us all (as if we needed it) of the bishop's sin. Without even asking us (we were rebuilding an old teacherage into a chapel of our own) he had planted on our island a prefabricated church, paid for by a Toronto parish and put up by off-island labor. The implication being that we were poverty-stricken heathens, to be condescended to by mainland church-goers and a Cooper Island bishop. His coming from Cooper was a sin in itself, because Cooper Island is big, rich, has blacktop roads, electric power, running water, and we are against it.

Mrs. Carpenter having established the case against the bishop, Mrs. Mildred Stonehenge, 92, rose to establish the case against Cooper Island. She did it by reading a bequest in her father's will. Dying in the early part of the century, he had left to Madronna Island the church silver (solid sterling) which he had brought out from England for his private chapel. The chapel had fallen into disuse, where-upon certain Cooper Island church members had come to Madronna *and stolen our silver*.

"And it's still in their church," added Mildred. "I saw it when I was being churched after my seventh." That must have been 50 years ago, but Mildred's memory can be as long as necessary. She offered to go along with a raiding party to identify Madronna's silver.

"Why didn't you protest at the time?" demanded Mr. Carpenter, who has a penchant for law and order. "I had the seven on my hands," replied Mildred blandly. They were in any case shouted down by Richard James, Elwy

127

Danson, Charlie Jo, Thorn Robertson and Captain O'Grady all offering their boats for the raid. It was decided to take Elwy Danson's boat, as the fastest, and Captain O'Grady (professional thief) as the leader, and the raiders rushed out of the hall with Mr. Carpenter crying forlornly in their wake, "Please don't smash the Cooper church door!" "I'll slip the lock with one of my credit cards," comforted Captain O'Grady. He has several hundred credit cards, all stolen.

Excitement still being high, the rest of us then adjourned to the church, where we auctioned off the kneelers. These kneelers have been particularly offensive to Mrs. Carpenter because they are covered with pious needlepoint embroidery, the work of the Toronto parishioners who donated the church. The kneelers brought $102 which will be sent to the Toronto church for its mission fund. The kneelers will remain where they are, which will be a comfort to Mrs. Carpenter, who has been one of the few attending the church but has had to do her praying upright.

The raiding party returned, rather disappointed at having encountered no resistance, but with the silver; and got on with tearing out the pre-fab pulpit and replacing it with the one Jed Peterson had carved for our chapel.

Today and tomorrow we're ripping the asbestos shingles off the roof and putting on Madronna cedar shakes.

The bishop won't recognize the church on Sunday. It won't be all his any more. It won't be all ours. It might even be God's. Full, for the first time, of sinners. All wondering if the bishop has called the RCMP.

ELINOR Filibruster has petitioned the provincial hydro again, demanding that a cable be laid from Braw Island to bring power to Madronna Island. Elinor has also demanded that it come aboard at the point just by her house, which is by no means the shortest way. Elinor has 22 signatures to her petition.

Elwy Danson has counter-petitioned to have the cable brought to a point just by his house, which would be a lot shorter but not short. Elwy always counters when Elinor petitions. He has 24 signatures to his petition.

Truth is, Elwy doesn't care if Madronna gets power or not. He has his own power plant. He has also done something he read about in a book. He has a deep-drilled well from which he pumps water with a half-horsepower motor. Water apparently gets warmer the further down in the earth it is. So it comes up warm and runs through pipes Elwy has laid under concrete in his floors, and warms the house. But going back down again the water is cold and picking up heat, so Elwy has run it through an insulated shed, and the cold water takes the heat out of the shed and turns it into a walk-in freezer.

I think the water must go down a different pipe from the one it comes up, but Elwy was out fishing when I started to write this and I couldn't ask him, and I know he lost the book that tells about it. It got under the concrete he was pouring over the pipes. So if you want to heat your house and have a deep freeze with the same water, you will have to get your own book.

Elwy is very generous with his deep freeze. He lets all the islanders keep their meat in it. The key is hung by the door and you are supposed to nip in and out fast, so as not to let the cold out. Even Elinor Filibruster keeps her sides of venison there. Police Sergeant Munro does not know that the shed is deep freeze, because most of what it contains is out-of-season venison.

But back to the power question. It has several layers. The top layer is that the provincial hydro has no intention of giving us power. It would have a screw loose if it did. There are only about 60 people on this island (some come and some go, Captain O'Grady on occasion to mainland jails), and they are scattered around a coastline of roughly 30 miles with a number living on tops of mountains.

Mr. Carpenter says we should keep the petitions moving in, however, because some time there might be a government damfool enough to lay a cable. Elinor Filibruster says it is a basic right of all Canadians to have electricity. Some islanders, mainly the mountain-top dwellers, say what do we want with power anyway? It would just attract all those mainland cottagers. And the rest of us, not having television, like a bit of live entertainment.

It will be pretty live with the hydro people sitting up on the Community Hall stage listening to Elinor Filibruster telling them they ought to spend a million or two to bring electricity to her doorstep, and Elwy being frugal about how it would cost only half a million to bring it to his, and Elinor shrilling at Elwy and Elwy baying at Elinor, and Elinor's husband saying, "Please dear," and Elwy's wife hauling on his coattails, and Mr. Carpenter deep-bassing about "Now, we're all reasonable people..."

And the hydro people will say, "Perhaps if the community could agree upon a single proposal..." After which we will all adjourn for gin cocktails (Captain O'Grady Bootleg).

The venison dinner may even be legal (if the season has opened).

IT was our first bridge day in September. We were at Helen Jessup's, down in June Harbor where the school perches on its own little knoll, when Mary Gathercole, the teacher, fell through the door screaming that the entire Madronna school had drowned.

The children had been diving off Harry Niblick's float by the north shore where the water is deep at all tides. Suddenly Mary saw, from the shore, that Johnny Cuthbert was missing. She shouted to the other children. The two biggest went in after him, and did not reappear.

Mary waded in herself. When she reached the float not a child was in sight. She swam under the float, sure the children had found airholes and were hiding there to scare her. There were no children. She dived to the bottom and became entangled in the weeds and nearly drowned. She found her strength going and swam back to shore and came screaming up for help.

Helen leaped to the phone to put out the disaster-come-all on the party line, and we ran to the beach, discarding clothing as we went.

We dived from the float and explored the weeds and came up for air and dived again. We spread out from the float and dived and rose and dived and rose. There were no small bodies.

"Try closer to the shore," cried Mrs. Carpenter, surfacing for another great labored breath. She is well past 60 and was diving in her bloomers.

The men began to arrive. There were around 25 of us diving now. The weeds were so dense that the children could be underneath.

At a time like that your body does what it must, but your mind is split. One half of mine knows that it is already too late. The other is crying and remembering and blaming me for bringing the twins to Madronna. It is seeing Michael going off to school that morning with his cowlick wet on his forehead from his efforts to suppress it; it will be suppressed forever now. It is seeing Judy bending down, laughing, to wave goodbye between her legs. Why has she taken to that habit? But she will never wave so again.

Mrs. Carpenter is in trouble. Mr. Carpenter and Harry Niblick tow her to the float. She is not breathing. "We can't go on wild like this," gasps Mr. Carpenter. "Harry, give them their stations." And he lifts his wife and presses the water from her and starts the kiss of life.

Harry is giving us our stations when suddenly, between float and shore, a head surfaces. It is Johnny Cuthbert. We are absolutely still. Another head surfaces. It is Lennie Danson. Three, seven, twelve. The entire Madronna school is bobbing out there, grinning at us. I don't know how I get my two, but they are in my arms and I am crying. Lettie and Elwy Danson have theirs, and they are crying. Mrs. Cuthbert is on the edge of the float, crying too, with Johnny over her knee and her hand coming down hard on the seat of his bathing trunks.

They meant it for a joke, the children explain, dabbing at our tears with small hands. There is this cave on the north shore with its opening under water but air above. They thought it would be fun to set Mrs. Gathercole up on the beach at recess and then vanish into the cave. They knew we were at Mrs. Jessup's, that the party line would bring the island. They had giggled in the cave, imagining our terror.

But now it is their terror. Mrs. Carpenter, fat kind Mrs. Carpenter, is lying there not breathing. The children are crying too. And oh thank God! when she finally takes an agonized breath of her own, and is sick.

More fun! More people killed! Growing up is hell. All round.

FROM the neck up old Les Chumley looks about 50. In other areas he is between 75 and 80. He won't tell but Richard James, by applying such guidelines as what were you doing when the First World War armistice was declared, what songs did you sing when you were Charlie Jo's age (instead of the tripe Charlie sings), who's your favorite actress, when did you put on your first pair of long pants?, has closed the limits to the satisfaction of the rest of us.

Les is comparatively young on top—at times you could take him for 40—because every day he does face exercises. I will give the exercises now to get them out of the way:

Hold each position with the muscles as hard as possible for slow count of six.

Turn your head parallel with your right shoulder, bring lower lip as close to your nose as possible. Hold. Same turned to left shoulder. For jowls.

Face front. Open mouth as wide as possible and raise eyebrows as far as possible. Same, but opening mouth as small as possible.

Swing mouth far to right. Then to left.

Do a kiss pucker, sucking in your cheeks.

Fill cheeks with air keeping mouth tight shut.

Tuck in corners of mouth, and holding, open mouth. Do between each of two above to fight whistle lines.

Bring lower lip as close to nose as possible.

Bring upper lip as close to chin as possible.

Press tongue hard against top of mouth.

Fight whistle lines again.

Muscles always as hard as possible. All exercises can be done in two minutes, with pauses between each.

It isn't so much the exercises that are interesting as people's reactions to them. Mr. Carpenter never did them; he doesn't care how old he looks. Mrs. Carpenter did them for three months (Les said that in three months you would look as though you'd had a facelift), and Mrs. Carpenter likes to try things. We took pictures of her from all angles first and, sure enough, at the end of three months she had changed so much she looked as though she'd had a facelift. After that she gave up face exercises and took up pottery. She doesn't care how old she looks either.

Some people say they don't do them, and do. They want us to think they're just naturally youthful looking. Elinor Filibruster says she did do them but they didn't work. Elinor did not do them; she can't discipline herself for even two minutes a day. Some other people do them when there's nothing to do—like when they're dummy at cards. Mary Gathercole, the teacher, makes the children do them with her every morning. She says this is to teach them good regular habits, like cleaning their teeth, but it also means that Mary does them (the children aren't going to need them for some time).

Most of the teenagers do them, although they don't need them yet either. They can't stand the thought of aging. Charlie Jo makes the rock band do them twice a day. This is partly because Charlie likes to be in command and partly because—although he has many important virtues—he is vain.

I do them in bed every morning, having pushed the pillow aside. They wake me up. Also I am vain.

Happily married (or commonlaw) couples either both do them or both don't do them. They are so secure with each other that looks don't matter between them, but the face they put to the world is united. There are not many of these couples.

Most people don't do them. Most people are lazy about non-essentials and—unlike Elinor—willing to let their faces admit it.

ORDINARILY we would not have given Susie house room. But it is very hard to bash a small animal who is sitting on your kitchen counter nibbling a piece of chocolate chip and does not duck when you advance to do the bashing. Not only does not duck but politely accepts, from your child's hand, another chocolate chip. Takes that and three other chocolate chips to her nest (from which we deduce that she has four children herself) and comes back to sit on hands, be tucked in shirt pockets (head poking out), and by the third day is answering calls of "Susie!"

We knew it was Susie and not one of her many friends and relatives because between the third and fourth chocolate chips we marked her ears with red ink.

By the end of a week she was a household familiar, taking her oatmeal porridge out of an ashtray on the breakfast table, but carrying the bacon rinds off to her family. Not willing to sit on laps but happy on all family shoulders or heads. Staying off strange shoulders and heads because the first strange shoulder she mounted belonged to Elinor Filibruster and Elinor was still screaming when she faded from hearing over the mountain.

By this time the dog and the two cats had been discouraged, with a rolled-up newspaper, from chasing Susie. The dog got the message fast and will even, with a mournful expression, permit her to sit on *his* head. (Susie must have her own individual smell because he does not extend similar accommodations to her friends and relatives.) The cats got the message all right, but disregard it except when actually caught stalking. That's cats all over. They know what you want but they do what they want. Our cats learned to roll over and jump through our hands and sit up and beg long before Tippy the dog did.

But they will not do it on command, even for catnip. It is a matter of principle. Sometimes, as a kindly gesture, they will do it *after* the catnip.

This makes it necessary to keep my bedroom door shut, if Susie is to survive, because that, we found out, is where she has her nest. It is in the bedding drawer of the bed-chesterfield.

And that made it all very difficult when Charlie Jo and Elwy Danson came to pick up the bed-chesterfield for the Joes' new home on the reserve.

On Madronna we pass around furniture as it is needed, and by this time I did not need the bed-chesterfield, having inherited a real bed from the Robertsons. So I had volunteered it for the Joes. But that was before I knew that Susie had a new family.

So when Charlie and Elwy turned up with the government truck, I asked if they could come back for the bed-chesterfield in—uh—three weeks. Because it was —uh—occupied just now.

"I didn't know you still had summer visitors," said Elwy.

"Occupied by what?" demanded Charlie, marching into my bedroom.

He looked at the bed-chesterfield, behind it, under it. Then, very carefully, he pulled out the bedding drawer. Then he started to laugh. He rolled on the floor laughing. After Elwy looked, he was rolling on the floor laughing too.

"We'll come back in three weeks," gulped Charlie. "We won't tell," gulped Elwy. And they staggered back to the truck still laughing themselves sick.

Really, some people are easily amused.

What's so funny about a small grey mouse proudly nursing four pink infants?

ONE thousand dollars. For no work. Simply for letting a mainland florist send in a crew in November to harvest the wild arbutus berry boughs on their two thousand or so wild acres. This is what the Carpenters had been offered. And it was the consensus of the island that only boneheads would refuse.

Not that it was any of the island's business. The offer was made by telephone and only the Carpenters ought to know about it. But at least Les Chumley was listening in, and the Carpenters were not at all surprised when we began to arrive with our advice to grab that mainland money.

You may not be acquainted with the arbutus. It is an elegant tree, shaped trunk and bough as though for a Japanese garden. It has large clusters of undistinguished flowers. These produce clusters of berries which in November turn a brilliant orange-red. Birds eat the berries; humans do not. But boughs of arbutus berries make much more artistic Christmas decorations than holly.

That was why the florist wanted them.

In commenting on the matter, we would merely have congratulated the Carpenters. But Les had reported that Jim Carpenter had not seemed to welcome the offer, had put it off, had finally said, "Well, call me again Saturday night. After I've got the mail out. I might be able to tell you then."

We had to get up there fast to tell him not to throw good money away.

"It would buy you a new battery pack," said Elwy Danson, who is saving to buy a new battery pack himself. A battery pack costs just as much and only lasts about a tenth as long as a power plant, which is unreasonable. Some scientist should do something about it. "You could get a new separator," Mrs. Cuthbert told Mrs. Carpenter, ignoring Mr. Carpenter. She and Mrs. Carpenter have a similar beef. Their milk separators have both broken down to the point where they will throw only very thick cream —so thick it has to be spooned—and the men have not got around to fixing them. "Out playing with their bull-dozers," says Mrs. Carpenter condescendingly. "Or you could get a decent kitchen table," said Elinor Filibruster, thus unconsciously uniting us all behind the Carpenters. Mrs. Carpenter's kitchen table is huge, made of long pine boards which she scours every day and sands once a month, and around which all of us feel at home. How dare Elinor!

But $1,000 is still an awful lot of money on Madronna. We were mystified. And all the more because Mrs. Carpenter was staying right out of it. That meant it was something that troubled Mr. Carpenter and she felt it was only fair to let him make his own decision. But what could it be?

"They wouldn't muck up the woods much," said Charlie Jo, "not more than next spring would fix." "I'd board the crew, if you'd rather not," said Mrs. Cuthbert. "Tell them you want $2,000," said Elwy.

No response.

So naturally we were all there Saturday night, taking coffee around the pine boards, when the florist called Mr. Carpenter. "No sir, I'm sorry," said Mr. Carpenter firmly. "I've decided you can't have the berries." And he hung up.

His eyes asked Mrs. Carpenter's forgiveness and got it. Then he looked shame-faced at the rest of us. "I just couldn't," he said. "Those berries are the wild birds' winter food."

WHEN the island wants to know something that will take a measure of investigation, it lays the chore on Richard James, our resident freelance writer who is a former journalist.

What the island wanted to know this time was what had happened to the government's project to restock Beachcomber Bay with lobsters. The island had not expected much of the project; it never expects much from government on anything, having had experience. But the government's fisheries boat had actually been observed putting lobsters into the water at Beachcomber's Bay four years ago, and by this time there should have been more lobsters. And there were not more lobsters.

One of our visiting ichthyologists says that Madronna is wrong for lobsters anyway, there are no lobsters in this area, there is no history of lobsters in this area, and he actually had to see a lobster pot coming up with a live lobster before he believed they *were* here. "Probably from a mistaken earlier stocking project," he said, declining to give ground. "I assure you that lobsters are not native to Madronna."

But we have to have them. Just a few anyway. Because although we have never made anything out of the lobsters themselves, we need them to validate our sales of lobster pots to mainlanders.

Richard took off, as requested, for the mainland, to find out why there were not more lobsters in Beachcombers Bay. He reported last night to the Community Club.

"I inquired first," said Richard, "at the headquarters of the fisheries department. They produced records which proved that, yes, four years ago last summer 500 lobsters, assorted sexes, were transported from Lady Port to Beachcombers Bay on Madronna Island, being in transit some five days. I believe they were seen going into Beachcombers Bay by Captain O'Grady and Johnny Cuthbert?''

"Right," said Captain O'Grady and Johnny Cuthbert.

"I then phoned the official of the fisheries department at Lady Port who had provided the lobsters. He said that, yes, he had procured the lobsters and placed them in salt water tanks and delivered them to the railway for transshipment to his colleague in charge of the fisheries boat based closest to Madronna.

"I then interviewed the said colleague who confirmed that, yes, he and his crew had transported the lobsters to Madronna and released them in Beachcomber Bay."

"Then why aren't they there?" demanded Captain O'Grady.

"Because," said Richard, "the Lady Port official of the fisheries department, knowing that the lobsters, having nothing else to eat in transit, would eat each other, had his men wire their claws so they couldn't eat anything. Owing, however, to some mischance in communication, the official of the fisheries department who received them at this end did not know that their claws were wired, and he and his men put them into Beachcomber Bay without removing the wires. About all that is left of them now is probably the wires."

As I said, Madronna does not expect much of governments.

Richard has arranged with a restaurant on the mainland, which gets its lobsters live, to sell us a couple of dozen for keeping in pots and producing when the ichthyologist or a visiting mainlander expresses disbelief in the existence of Madronna lobsters.

ON Madronna, if you can build one road to serve two families, you do, because it can take 10 years to persuade the government to pay for a second road.

When our road foreman, Jim Carpenter, was carelessly instructed on the telephone by the district foreman to build a road to the Brown place, the entire island combined to do so within days. The telephone went down right after the original instruction, making an honest mistake possible, and we kept it down until the road was through to *our* Brown place. The road to *our* Brown place connects the two sides of the island. What the district foreman had had in mind was a road to the *new* Brown place. The new Browns are friends of a prominent politician.

They haven't mixed with us much. During the summer they came over in their boat and anchored in their bay. They brought their own supplies with them and their own friends; and according to Charlie Jo, who passes their bay on the way to his bay, they had some fine parties. They would have had even better parties if they had a pipeline to Captain O'Grady's bootleg gin. They will never have a pipeline.

But, come autumn, the district foreman instructed Mr. Carpenter to put a road through to the new Brown place. The new Browns wanted a lodge built during the winter (not, naturally, using lumber from the Madronna mill) and they wanted a road in so that building materials could be trucked from the government wharf.

Fine. We wanted a road in that general area, too. The Jos' new house on the reserve is up—but it will be easier to visit them in all weathers if there's a road. The Community Club and the chief of the reserve decided that the road would follow the line between the reserve and the

Browns' property, half on each, to just back of the waterfront, where one branch would be taken in behind the Jos' place and another in behind the Brown's building site.

And so it was done. Elwy Danson was paying off his taxes, and there was no blasting involved, so he brought his bulldozer and punched the new roads through in no time.

Whereupon the new Browns arrived and raised holy hell. They had wanted a nice private road—at public expense—meandering through the forest, making a graceful curve around each big tree. Whereas Elwy had meticulously followed the property line, knocking down a collection of balsam, pine, maple and oak. The Browns were really quite impolite, in the store, in front of the entire community. They said they would be in touch with the district foreman, the provincial deputy minister, the minister and the Premier. They said they were going to sue Mr. Carpenter and Elwy for knocking down their trees.

They will return on Saturday with, we hope, the Premier. Because they are going to need a bulldozer, and there are only two bulldozers on Madronna, and one of them is in Jarge Gallagher's retirement home for old machinery and he never lends it to strangers. The other is Elwy's. And Elwy has taken it out and done some more work. The road to the Jos' is still clear. But on the other half, supported by deadfalls, gravel and all the boulders Mr. Carpenter's blasting could provide, is the forest.

Elwy has put the Browns' trees back up.

DAN Masterson got the hull of the Elsey in his glasses with the first dawn light, and the only boat he could send right away was Captain O'Grady's Sweeper. The only crew was Elwy Danson, who was booming up logs in the cove.

It was bad out there, waves eight to ten feet and breaking two ways with the gale cutting across a heavy tide. They didn't know it was the Elsey until they were almost on her. She's an old deephulled sailer, turned to power, and then put back to sail this summer when the engine ran out. When they came into her lee they saw that one man was still hanging on—Buz Thomson.

Buz saw them and seemed to shout and let go his hold and tried to swim toward them. He took two strokes, and then he went down or a wave broke over him, and he was gone. The tide must have taken him because it was maybe an hour, and well in toward the island, before his yellow lifejacket glimmered at them through a wave. The Captain got the Sweeper stern to, where the freeboard is least, and Elwy had to crawl along the deck or the wind would have taken him. He got a grip on Buz's lifejacket. But he couldn't get him over the stern, not in that sea.

In the end the little Captain had to lash the wheel and get down alongside Elwy with a pikepole. Getting the pikepole into the lifejacket the Captain slashed Buz's face, but in that battering sea it couldn't be helped. They waited until it lifted Buz towards them and then they heaved and he came aboard suddenly, tearing his torn face on the guard rail as he passed. The captain lay under him while Elwy pressed the water out of him, and then went back to the wheel as Elwy started mouth to mouth respiration.

The Captain had to stop Elwy's count on Buz when they

found the next one, young Syd Cuthbert, and the next, Joe Elsey, and the next, young Bud Elsey. Sergeant Munro came alongside in the police launch then. Elwy pointed at their cargo, and held up four fingers, and pointed at the sea and held up one finger. Because Ronny Patchel was still out there. "He'll have to tow him," the Captain shouted to Elwy above the storm. "He'll never get him over that stern alone." And then the Sweeper had to head home because she had cracked a seam and was taking a lot of water.

Elwy stopped trying to blow life back into Buz, it wasn't any use, all those hours it never had been, and started pumping. He pumped nearly nine miles down the coast of Madronna, and in the heavy sea the bodies fell loosely about the deck, like sacks of wet laundry, anchored each by a foot to a bollard or the railing, but curiously mobile. Buz kept falling against Elwy where he worked at the pump. His eyes, strange for a man who had drowned, were wide open. Perhaps his heart had given out first.

When they came round Point Ernest into quiet water, Elwy reached over and closed Buz Thomson's eyes.

It was 500 yards, perhaps, to the government wharf, and the whole of Madronna waiting for them, a silent huddle of men and women and children. The Captain and Elwy felt shame at what they brought them. The silent men flung down like dolls by untidy children. They all seemed to have shrunk, somehow, from the size of life. Even a fat man like Buz Thomson lies flat when he's dead. But their big sea-boots were enormous. Little men lying there in big boots that had walked a deck, trod the paths of the living, tramped mud across the kitchen floors of home.

WHEN the Elsey went over in the autumn's first gale, Captain O'Grady in his Sweeper, with Elwy Danson, brought in four of the dead. Police Sergeant Munro brought in the fifth. The island met them at the wharf and sent them up to the Carpenters' to be alone together and get drunk and weep. Any remote mining or fishing community knows that it is necessary for rescuers who have failed to do this.

In such places possible disaster always lives next door, and the outside world is usually too far away to get there in time, and the grief and the guilt must be faced and separated.

To some extent we knew what had to be sorted, because Dan Masterson at the lighthouse had had his glasses on them all the way. He had seen that one man had remained with the wreck when the Captain and Elwy had reached it, and that he had left it and tried to swim to them and been lost in the wild sea until it was too late for them to save him. For this the Captain and Elwy would at first feel guilt, but in the end they would know that it was Buz Thomson who had lost his own life. In an accident at sea you stay with the boat.

Sergeant Munro had a greater burden. He had received the Mayday when he was alone in the police launch off Tooley Island and had set off immediately for the wreck. He would have felt that 20 minutes lost could be a life lost. But he would know now and forever that it was a mistake not to have gone into Tooley and picked up a second hand. In that sea one man could not haul a drowning man aboard. No life would have been saved if he had followed the proper procedure, for they were all hours dead before he reached the scene. But he had had to tow Ronny Patchel nine miles behind the launch before he reached the lee of Point Ernest, and he did not then know if Ronny was alive or dead. If alive, he had lost him; if dead, he had done him an indignity.

Madronna would not say that at the inquest, but Sergeant Munro would.

The inquest would not hear about the broader guilt of the island, for there were no facts, except the fact of seaweed in the Elsey's rigging. Which said to us that she had left herself, in the face of a gale warning, without enough searoom for sail, and been blown over on the northern reef, and swept out again on the turning tide.

Joe and Bud Elsey were drowned from her. Buz Thomson. Young Syd Cuthbert. Ronny Patchel. She was an old boat, built as a sailer, and many years ago turned to power. Joe put her back to sail last spring because his engine had packed in and he could not afford a new engine and the rising cost of fuel. He had sought the cheapness of the wind, and the price of his ignorance, and the ignorance of the island, had been five of our lives.

This island knows nothing about sailing, it has only working boats. The Carpenters had lent Joe the money to buy sails. Richard James had got him a book about sailing. Elwy Danson had found a visiting yachtman to go out with the crew and give them some tips. We had known that they were not first-rate boatmen, of any kind, that they were a happy bunch of adventuring clowns, whom we loved. We had known that sailing is different from power-boating, requiring different knowledge and different skills. But we had let them trifle merrily, all summer, with the sea.

So we had all of us our guilt. For we knew the sea, and that it is vast and violent and cannot care.

THE Macaw is staying with us at present. The Macaw usually journeys around with the Madronna folk-rock band in its pedal-car, sitting on the top of the windshield to hurl insults at passing motorists, and walking ahead of the band into performances. During performances it sits on the shoulder of Charlie Jo, who leads the band, and contributes to the cacophony.

At present it is resting, as they say in the theatrical world, because it bit Charlie Jo's latest girlfriend and she demanded that it be fired. We (Madronna, that is) suspect that further down the road she intends to detach Charlie from his family, Madronna Island and probably the folk-rock band. Madronna is placing bets that she will not succeed, and only off-islanders will take our money. They don't know Charlie Jo. Mrs. Carpenter finds it hard to discern any flaws in Charlie, but she felt it necessary to tell him—in the store where all his friends and relatives could hear her—that he was leading the chit on. He listened respectfully and then took me out to present me to The Macaw.

I can almost sympathize with the chit. There was no doubt that The Macaw had to be brought to approve of me, not me of The Macaw.

First we had to drive to my place in the pedal-car. This meant pedalling up and down two mountains, which is very hard work. They were kind enough to let me steer, but I am not surprised that the original owner of the pedal-car kicked it off the wharf.

Then The Macaw had to be introduced to our animals. Mr. Macaw, meet Tippy the Dog. Mr. Macaw, meet Blackie the Cat, meet Tiger the Cat. Mr. Macaw, forgive Blackie for taking a swipe at you. Mr. Macaw, LEAVE MY

CAT'S TAIL ALONE. Mr. Macaw, your stand will be here. NO, you cannot sit on the back of the rocking chair. All right then, just wait till Coonie the raccoon catches you at it. Mr. Macaw, this is the maple tree up which you may spend your afternoons.

In high dudgeon, in fact, he spent the first day and night up the maple tree.

The Macaw has now come to accept the humans in the house. He condescends to let us feed him, open doors for him and answers when we call him down from his maple tree. He will not come down for visitors. He will sit at the top of the tree and curse them.

He has chased Narcissus the visiting peacock back to the Cuthberts', removing most of Narce's tailfeathers on the way. He has totally subdued Tippy the Dog and Blackie the Cat. He spends much of his indoor time on the back of the rocking chair. When Coonie, the three-legged coon, arrives through the kitchen window, there is a flurry of bad language, some flying feathers and fur, and Coonie retrieves the rocking chair. Between Mr. Macaw and Tiger the Cat there is the mutual respect of disreputable and equal adversaries. They both want the wooden Buddha.

The Buddha, which is one and a half inches tall, was stolen by Tiger from the Carpenters' and carried over here—a good five miles—in her mouth. Tiger takes it around with her. When she is hunting she leaves it on the mantel. The Macaw steals it. When Tiger returns The Macaw sidles along the back of the rocking chair clutching the Buddha in his left claw. Tiger stares at him. He gets all huffy and nervous. Suddenly Tiger lunges and takes the Buddha back. The Macaw makes a lot of racket, but he never hurts Tiger. Tiger never hurts him. But the Buddha is beginning to show wear.

So are we.

ONE of our visiting zoologists says that it is a mistake to personalize animals because then you attribute human characteristics to them which is all wrong because they don't have them. This zoologist always comes accompanied by an ancient black Scottie who sits between his feet and growls for his porridge. When the cook (me) put brown sugar on the porridge the Scottie knocked the bowl over. As the zoologist was cleaning up, he explained that his Scottie (Elmer) prefers white sugar. He did not seem to view this as personalizing Elmer.

As a zoologist he undoubtedly knows much more about animals in general than Madronna Islanders do, and is probably right that they do not have human individuality. But Coonie, our visiting three-legged coon, seems to have mastered the human idea of rising expectations.

Coonie used to be content with a slice of white bread. Then one day Michael gave him a slice of brown bread. After that Coonie would have nothing to do with anything *but* brown bread. Then Judy slipped him a piece of her buttered brown toast. From that day Coonie rejected anything but buttered brown toast. And last week, while I was at the bridge club and Johnny Cuthbert was baby-sitting, they tried him out on buttered brown toast with blackberry jam, strawberry jam and honey.

Coonie prefers honey.

So now we have a dependent raccoon who insists on buttered brown toast with honey. If they try advancing his diet any further I'll put them all on bread and water until these rising expectations are flattened. It is perhaps informative that the bread he hands to his mate through the kitchen window (she hangs onto the drainpipe outside) can be any old bread.

Jenny, the Cuthberts' Clydesdale, may not have human characteristics either, but she certainly knows about loneliness. Since they bought her she has never seen another horse except her own colts, which are bred by artificial insemination. When they are taken away to be sold, she goes into what, if she were a human mother, would be called deep depression. She stands in the far corner of the field with her head down, and for the longest time not even Johnny Cuthbert can persuade her to eat or drink.

A couple of months ago, though, Johnny sneaked home a fox terrier he had been given by a beachcomber. He hid the terrier in the barn while he went about preparing his mother to accept another dog. But he never had to. When Timson the terrier went out with Johnny to try to persuade Jenny to take at least a drink (she had just lost her latest colt), the tiny terrier and the huge horse touched muzzles. They have not been separated since.

Jenny sleeps standing up, and Timson sleeps with his front paws around her left front foot. They are both kind to Johnny, but it is plain that he is displaced in their affections by each other.

It is proof that Johnny is a good kid (he is generally referred to as a young devil) that instead of being jealous he went right out and cadged a half-grown border collie pup for the Mastersons' Percheron mare, who was also alone. That friendship, too, has taken off like a forest fire.

The Cuthberts and the Mastersons are convinced that once the energy crisis gets bad enough there will be a great demand for draft horses.

Johnny plans to see that they all have dogs for friends.

Mary Gathercole, the teacher, had the children disciplined last year to leave their rubber boots by the door and go about the schoolhouse in moccasins made by Charlie Jo's Grandmother out of deer skin. But she has a problem this year. They're in loggers' boots. And loggers' boots lace. They don't pull off easy, with one child hanging onto the doorknob and a mate pulling.

Mary foresaw the problem and sent all the parents notes asking us not to equip our children with loggers' boots. But you can't fight fashion. And fashion in the islands this year is loggers' boots.

Actually, loggers' boots are much more practical for climbing up and down mountains, which almost all of the children have to do. They have the treads of a tractor. But they certainly do tramp a lot of mud over a floor.

Mrs. Carpenter said, "Make the children sweep the mud out."

Mary, who took a summer course in the psychology of teaching, approached the question more subtly. She suggested to the children that Grandma Jo would be hurt if she thought they were not using the moccasins she had made for them.

The children approached the question directly. They went and asked Grandma Jo if she was hurt. Grandma Jo was bemused. She said if they didn't want to wear the moccasins at school, why didn't they take them home? Grandma Jo was wearing loggers' boots.

Do not think that Mary was letting the loggers' boots be *worn* in school. Any psychology she may have imbibed in her summer course is but frill about an iron belief in discipline. The loggers' boots were being taken off at the school door and replaced with Grandma's moccasins, but since the smaller children couldn't lace and unlace it was taking a lot of Mary's time and eating into class time.

Mrs. Carpenter said, ''Make the big kids do the lacing and unlacing for the little kids.'' This was in the store on a Saturday. Mrs. Carpenter was wearing loggers' boots.

As a matter of fact, more and more adult Madronna feet are feeling acutely embarrassed in Mary Gathercole's presence. (Not Mrs. Carpenter's; Mrs. Carpenter's feet wouldn't recognize embarrassment any more than any of the rest of her.) But loggers' boots grip, they fit nice and firm around the ankles. When the mud is three or four inches deep as it is right now after that three-day downpour we needed to make the woods safe from fire, they march right straight through.

And if you have to go out to feed the chickens, in to put the beans to soak, out to pull onions for egg sandwiches, in to make the sandwiches, out to throw rocks at the mink who is hanging around the chicken run, in to make sure that four-year-old Dorene has her loggers' boots laced and tied, out to wave goodbye to Michael, Judy and Dorene as they set off for school (Mary is really a marvel of a teacher in many ways, she takes even the three-year-olds because she thinks they should learn to socialize), in to have a collecting-the-mind cup of coffee and it isn't yet 9 a.m., well, you don't stop to take off your loggers' boots.

Last Saturday Mr. Carpenter, who is the postmaster, reported that a box came from the catalogue for Mary Gathercole. He thinks our feet may soon be at ease. The computer had put the bill on the outside.

Loggers' boots.

I SAW this stuffed raccoon in a store window," said Richard James, relaxing over a coffee in our kitchen, "and I thought it would be fun to get Coonie's goat by putting it on the back of his rocking chair. So I went in to ask the price. Do you know what they wanted?" He paused for effect. "One hundred and twenty-one dollars!"

"Don't know where to put their money," said Mrs. Carpenter.

"It wasn't even a genuine stuffed raccoon," said Richard. "It was one of those plush things."

"I don't think you'd get a rise out of Coonie with that," said Mr. Carpenter. "So far as I can tell, animals don't go by look. They go by smell. It wouldn't have smelled right."

We all looked at Coonie, who was allowing Michael to use the seat of his rocking chair. Michael is only 10 and his head does not rise high enough to get in the way of Coonie's view. Coonie was eating grapes that Richard had brought back for him. Now he stuck down a paw as he had done once or twice before and offered a grape to Michael. This might not strike you as generosity, but in a raccoon to a human it is virtually unheard of. Michael accepted the grape—no nonsense about washing it for either of them —and considered Connie.

"Would Coonie be worth $121?" he asked.

"I wouldn't think so," said Richard judicially. "After all, he's only got three paws. You'd have to knock off about a quarter for that. And then of course, you'd have to kill and stuff him."

"Think you're being funny?" demanded Michael, bounding out of the rocking chair.

"No," said Richard, "thought you were."

And while the child bristled and the man didn't, we all

paused for a moment and looked at the proposition. How much is Coonie worth? A wild, three-legged raccoon, who comes in most evenings by the window above the sink left unlatched for him, takes a piece of brown bread from the breadbox, indicates that somebody had better toast it and put butter and honey on it, and takes his place on the back of the kitchen rocker while the chore is done. Who is clever with his paws and absolutely untrustworthy when it comes to food. You ever come home to find the cookies, two cakes and a pudding half-eaten and otherwise all muddled up on the kitchen floor? We had to have Captain O'Grady put locks on the food cupboards. We wouldn't be surprised if Coonie found the key and unlocked them.

He bites people he doesn't like. People he does like (and you can tell if you're liked by whether he'll let you sit in his rocking chair) he will sometimes reach down and pat on the cheek. He will occasionally lie around the necks of three people he likes—Michael, Richard and Charlie Jo. He will wrestle with the dog, one cat and the children; not with Tiger the cat, who has made it clear she's in charge around here. He will not lie on laps.

Well, once he did, when it was late at night and the person sitting in his rocker was in deep grief. Just quite quietly. But it didn't prevent him, the next day, from walking through six of her pumpkin pies.

We watched him eating his grapes. The wild come indoors. Down to two grapes, which he contemplated, finally offering the smaller to Michael.

"You better watch it, Coonie," said Michael, who at 10 is catching on, "or we'll turn you into a fur piece."

IF you can play the piano, and if you should visit Madronna, and if you should be so unfortunate as to be invited to Elinor Filibruster's for a musical evening, you may now play her piano.

For the last few months we have had to warn off-islanders who could play the piano that if they went to Elinor's they couldn't. It would have exposed Irwin Hoffstater to the terrible Elinor Filibruster wrath. You see, in delivering it, Irwin let the piano fall off the back of the government truck.

The way it happened was this. Elinor, who cannot play the piano, bought it at an auction on Cooper Island for purely status purposes and had it conveyed to Madronna on the SS Lady Lucinda. The Lucy's captain picked it up with the ship's crane and set it down on the back of the government truck. Irwin should have roped it, but he forgot. All went well enough as he drove straight up the road, but when he took the sharp turn at the Community Hall, the piano fell off on its back.

Several islanders (Elinor not among them) were standing on the Community Hall porch and went into instant action. The women rushed down to the store to engage Elinor in extended conversation. The men slapped the sides back on the piano, lifted it on the truck and delivered it to Elinor's. They set it close to the wall in the living-room, and fortunately there were no scratches on the visible parts that could not be blamed on the captain of the Lucy.

Richard James, who *can* play the piano, tried it out and it was awful. Some of the keys didn't sound at all and those that did were hideously off. He and Charlie Jo (who can also play the piano) were immediately put into slings, left hand and right. And Charlie Jo was sent up the mountain to bring down our muscial recluse whose name we do not know but who sometimes answers to Silby. Silby is very shy, scratches a living by making recorders and was the only person on Madronna who could possibly mend the piano.

It was a long and painful process. First Charlie had to persuade Silby to come at a certain time on a certain day. And then one of us had to invite Elinor and her husband out for lunch or dinner or whatever. Elinor is the kind of guest who tells you that you put too much onion in the chicken dressing, the zucchinis should have been casseroled instead of steamed, she doesn't really care for baked potatoes and you must come over some day and she will teach you how to make pie crust.

You will understand Madronna's affection for Irwin when I explain that Elinor (and her husband) were invited out for no fewer than three lunches and 11 dinners. At each one of which she explained what a grief it was to her that no visitors had come to the island who could play her piano and that those two uncouth louts, Richard James and Charlie Jo, had both picked fights with Poor Pet (her husband) and refused to darken her door.

But last night (while the Filibrusters were taking dinner at the Carpenters) Silby gave us a concert. We had to hide in the bushes to hear it, because Silby can't bear an audience. But the thing works.

So if you come to Madronna and can play the piano and Elinor invites you up (she will probably offer you pie with crust like leather) you are now free to give a performance.

But please avoid middle C. Even Silby couldn't make it strike.

NOTHING like a splendid new resource to start the battles.

The new resource is the lake in a cup near the top of one of our mountains which was created by Charlie Jo's teen-age government-grant crew, who cleared the basin, and Elwy Danson, who put the dam in with his bulldozer. The lake, with the heavy rains we've been having, is already full to overflowing. It is overflowing into a series of pools dipping down the mountain which were dammed off by Jarge Gallagher, who actually took *his* bulldozer out of retirement to make them.

The argument, over every kitchen table and at two meetings now of the Community Club, is what to do with the water.

Most of the old-timers say, why do anything? The lake will keep wells from running dry. Isn't that enough? Elwy Danson and Thorn Robertson want to harness the water, as it rushes down the mountain, to make electricity. Other people, whose homes happen to be near the water course, want to pipe the water in. Richard James says he sees no reason why we can't do both. Richard knows absolutely nothing about either electricity or plumbing but is confident that somebody does and that he can find out.

Charlie Jo and his gang are up at the other end of the island, trying to catch the beavers Charlie's Indian relatives brought in to maintain the dams. The beavers were put in storage in a marshy area, which has a slow-moving creek ambling through it. The beavers seem to like it where they are and have so far declined to be tempted into any live-traps. The people at that end of the island like the beavers where they are, because by damming up *that* stream, they have stabilized surrounding wells. There has been snarling about any contemplated transfer of the beavers, which their neighbors now refer to as *our* beavers.

Charlie Jo and Yoste McMurtry are said to have had fisticuffs over the matter. Charlie says certainly not and Yoste has a black eye, which means that Charlie won. The fight, that is. The beavers are still holding the territory.

There are sub-battles. If anything at all is done with the water from the lake, there will be a lot of work needed and some money. We all know who will work, who won't work and who can't work. And we all know who won't pay and who can't pay. The workers and payers don't mind subsidizing those who can't. They have strong views about subsidizing those who could but won't.

They also know full well that the loafers and the misers will steal either water or electricity or both. To deal with this situation they are making plans which everybody knows won't work because Mr. Carpenter, having both worked and paid, will say, "But you can't cut even slobs off from water or power."

Nobody, except Elinor Filibruster, wants the government in: the island would be flooded by civil servants, standards would be required which we do not feel are needed, the health department would insist on chlorination, the electricity people would make us put up poles to carry the electrical wires (which we intend to hang from trees) and it would all cost so much that we would get neither water nor power.

Elinor Filibruster has written the government to protest that the rest of us are upsetting the ecology of the island. Mr. Carpenter, the postmaster, has taken the precaution of removing her letter from the mail.

ED Foulkes was deputy returning officer this time. Flo Davis was his clerk. Whatever the principles governing appointment of these officials elsewhere, on Madronna they are those laid down by Mrs. Carpenter:

Everybody shall, as a public duty, take turns serving as deputy returning officer or clerk. Except those who can't be trusted. If somebody actually needs the pay for the job, that person shall be deputy returning officer, which pays more. At least the clerk must know how to do the job.

Ed Foulkes needed the money because a mink had got into his rabbit hutches and killed the lot, and he had to restock. That is one of the endearing characteristics of minks which probably result in there being no Save the Minks organizations: they kill, not to eat, but for the pleasure of it.

Richard James gave me a ride over in his boat. We were the first voters.

"Look!" said Ed, before we were properly through the door. "Look at this!" We went round the table and looked. Ed's finger was at a name part way down the printed list of voters. Edwin Robert Foulkes, it said.

"Edwin Robert Foulkes," said Ed. "I never saw it printed before."

"You fold the ballot like this, Ed," said Flo, folding it, "and then you hand it to the voter." She handed it to me. "And when she comes back from voting she gives it to you and you tear off this piece and put the rest in the ballot box." I went to vote behind the piano.

"Looks nice, doesn't it?" said Ed.

"Certainly does," said Richard, as Flo folded his ballot. "You've got an impressive name, Ed."

"Oh no!" cried Ed to Flo who was drawing a line

through my name on the list. "You can't spoil it like that."

"But I have to," said Flo. "I have to draw a line through the name of each voter who votes. So nobody can vote twice."

"We'll remember," said Ed. "We won't let anybody vote twice."

"I once read," said Richard, from behind the other side of the piano, "that only a million Canadians ever see their names in print. That includes birth and death notices and the police blotter. They must have overlooked the voters' list."

"And credit cards," said Flo. "No, Ed," as Ed accepted my folded ballot and opened it. "It's a secret ballot. You don't read anybody's ballot."

"Don't you think you should have voted for Mr. Carpenter?" said Ed to me. "Elwy Danson's a nice young chap, but it's Mr. Carpenter who knows."

"Mr. Carpenter isn't running," said Flo, capturing the ballot, refolding it and putting it in the ballot box. "No, Ed, I told you you mustn't read the ballots," rescuing Richard's ballot.

"You voted for Elwy too," said Ed reproachfully, but with most of his attention on the voters' list, from which Richard was now eliminated. "I think that spoils it. Putting a line through a man's name. We could just remember."

"But we've got to send everything back to Cooper Island," explained Flo, "and they can't remember there."

"Hey Jim!" cried Ed, as Mr. Carpenter came through the door. "Come and look at this! Edwin Robert Foulkes!"

"He was very distressed," Flo told us later, "that we had to send the voters' list back to Cooper. But Edwin Robert Foulkes went unblemished. He didn't vote."

"He would have voted for Mr. Carpenter anyway," said Richard.

THE pick-up supper was at my place, after the painting bee at the Community Club. When we all arrived in the Government truck, the corned beef was ready in the Dutch oven, the baked potatoes and squash had done well with the oven door just open. And the kitchen floor was covered with six inches of shredded newspaper. Also the downstairs bedrooms, the bathroom, the hall and bits and pieces throughout the house.

"It was those cats," said Elinor Filibruster with distaste. Those cats were certainly looking dead beat, curled up in the seat of the kitchen rocker with their paws around each other's necks.

"It's lucky you've got help," said Mr. Carpenter. "Where's the garbage bags? It must have taken them hours."

"Cats don't usually stick to a job," said Mrs. Carpenter, anchoring the lip of a garbage bag with her foot and starting to sweep. "I bet it was Tiger that started it. She's the smart one."

"I can't stand tabbies," said Elinor, moving out of the way of Mrs. Carpenter's broom.

"But it'd be Blackie that kept the job moving," said Richard James, down on his hands and knees shovelling. "He's the conscientious one. He's not what I'd call an efficient cat. When he tries to jump over a fence he always hits it. But when he starts a job he finishes it. Remember that time he had eight dead rats laid out for your inspection when you got home from the boat? How many newspapers did you have saved up, anyway?"

"Eight piles, each about four feet high," I told him, bringing in the snowshovel. "Doe Kelly and the Foulkes, they don't take a newspaper, so I keep extras to start their

161

fires, too.''

"Pet," said Elinor to her husband, "would you push those cats out of that rocking chair? I've got such a crick from painting I'll have to sit down."

"Just lift your feet," murmured Mrs. Carpenter, "as somebody else sweeps past. Myself," raising her voice, "I like tabbies. But I'd like to know how Blackie kept her at it."

"He probably bit her," I said. "He does sometimes. Especially if she's been pranking in the bushes with Shaughnessy."

"Shaughnessy!" said Mr. Carpenter. "I bet he helped. That would account for it."

"Shaughnessy," said Richard, jumping in his garbage bag to pack it down, "weighs 26 pounds. He can't get through the cat door."

"He got stuck once," said Michael, my twin son. "Judy"—his twin—"had to put a towel around his head and push from in front and I had to pull on his back legs from behind. And when we got him out he bit me." He looked at his thumb. We all—except Elinor—looked at our thumbs. The mark of Shaughnessy.

"I cannot understand," said Elinor, "why somebody doesn't shoot that Shaughnessy."

Shaughnessy probably cannot understand why somebody doesn't shoot her. They neither of them realize that they are collectors' items.

We—Elinor of course excepted—filled 19 garbage bags, packed down, with the newspapers shredded by Tiger and Blackie. Tiger and Blackie, bounced from the rocking chair, had taken their proud and weary selves to the warm spot behind the stove.

Elinor said the delay had made the corned beef dry.

WE had to use the stand-by coffin again yesterday. Not for burying. In the funeral we have had since the Community Club opened the new graveyard—to beat mainland dying costs—the coffin was made by Jed Peterson assisted by Charlie Jo. Narrow at the feet, widening for the shoulders and rounded above the head. Straight out of old pictures of witches and goblins. In fact, straight out of Sussex, England, where Jed learned carpentry from his father, and making the village coffins was just part of the trade.

The stand-by coffin, with necessary appurtenances, sits on the rafters in the government garage.

Yesterday it was needed because Colin Close, being well tanked, ran his truck off the Mount Porter road. Elwy Danson, who was following behind him with Irwin Hoffstater, sent Irwin for the coffin and help, and clambered down to find Colin out cold and shedding blood all over but in particularly nasty spurts from a compound-fractured leg. Elwy used his shirt for a tourniquet on the leg and got Colin out and away from the truck because you have to make your choices. It's risky for one man to move a compound-fracture, but in an accident like that you can never tell if the gas tank will blow.

Colin was still bleeding badly when we arrived—the Carpenters and Irwin and Charlie Jo and me. Richard James had gone down to the wharf to warm up his speedboat, which is the fastest on the island.

We got out some of the appurtenances, rolls of adhesive and Kotex—the thick kind. Handy stuff. Sterile in its box, soaks up a lot of blood, and taped firmly in place makes a good pressure bandage. Mrs. Carpenter and I Kotexed Colin's face and head and shoulders—he'd gone through the windshield and been yanked back by the steering wheel but the glass hadn't got his jugular. At the other end the men were using another of the appurtenances—a flat board—to make the broken leg immobile. Strapping it down with adhesive.

Then we got the coffin as flat as possible—not very flat, we were on a mountainside—and got half on one side of Colin and half on the other, with our arms straight out under him, and lifted him into the coffin. The coffin has straps in it now, because a lot of the accidents seem to happen on mountains and you don't want the casualty slumping around. So we strapped him in, leaving the board off his face and off the fracture, because the tourniquet had to be loosened off from time to time. The rest of us got badly scratched by blackberry bushes, getting him back to the road, but Colin in the coffin was as safe, in the circumstances, as he could be.

He was safer in the coffin on the boat too. Because when the sea's kicking up, as it was yesterday, a speedboat going all out slaps you around so much you have to keep your teeth parted or they'll break each other. But you can't go slow with a bad case, and he can't fall out of a coffin. Mrs. Carpenter phoned ahead to tell the Cooper Island hospital to watch for the boat putting into its wharf.

We knew how the men would carry Colin off. High on their shoulders and, if they weren't too beat, whistling the Dead March.

It drives the Cooper Island doctors wild, especially the psychiatrist.

What, he always demands of these brutal Madronna Islanders, do they think they're doing to the patient's psyche?

JASON Danson and his trawler have been fishing out of the mainland for the last two weeks, but we think his marriage to Holly Jopdale is coming off all right. Holly has consented to having her wedding dress made. She was not at the first dressmaking session because she was helping her future brother-in-law, Elwy Danson, boom up logs.

She wants the dress to have tucks, crocheted inserts, old-fashioned drawn work, and to be of pure white cotton. Her landlady, Mildred Stonehenge, who is 92, says it ought to be scarlet. "I suppose," she said to us, wielding her crochet hook, "that you think I don't know she and Jason have been shacked up at my place for months."

"Yes we know," said Mrs. Carpenter, showing the younger set how to do drawn work. "You told us."

"At least 50 times," said Lettie Danson, laying the pattern out on the fine white cotton. "And you dumped a bucket of water over Jason's head when he was coming out the last morning. It may have scared him off for good."

"Nothing scares a Danson off," said Mildred. "If anybody cuts and runs it'll be Holly. I know she was trying to get a job off-island as a teacher."

"How do you know?" demanded Mrs. Carpenter.

"I just happened to glance at some correspondence she left lying around on the dining-room table," said Mildred. (Holly rents the dining room and former butler's pantry in Mildred's decrepit mansion and after the wedding she and Jason will also take over one of the bedrooms. Mildred says they're not going to live in sin in any of *her* bedrooms. The bed-chesterfield doesn't seem to count.) "But I think," went on Mildred, "that she was just making noises. You don't apply for a teacher's job these days if you expect to get one."

"I bet she made noises if she caught you at her letters," said Lettie.

"She didn't catch me," said Mildred. "She was out in the kitchen trying to make steak and kidney pie because Jason likes it. She gets taken that way after they've had a good fight. What that girl doesn't know about cooking would feed the island. I had to show her how to chop an onion."

"Jason can make his own kidney pie," said Lettie. "He often does."

"I told her," said Mildred, "I told her, 'You'll never be the cook Jason is. But at least you could learn the plain things. If he helps you with the shakesplitter'—he's buying her a shakesplitter for a wedding present, trust a Danson—'you ought to help him with the cooking.' Mind you, she'll be no good on the trawler, gets seasick. I will say, though, she's got a good eye with a rifle. Dropped a buck last night that I had in my flashlight."

"Mildred," said Mrs. Carpenter. "You saw the notice Sergeant Munro put up about pit-lamping. Two months that man on Cooper Island got."

"Jack-lighting, Holly calls it. Foreign. That man on Cooper was a visitor. The sergeant didn't mean islanders, and Holly will make an islander. But Jason," said Mildred, "should have been here to butcher that buck. It's a heavy job. Cold feet, that's what's keeping him on the mainland. Warm your cold feet on each other's backs, that's what I told them. Where's the tape to measure this lace? I still say it shouldn't be white."

"Mildred," asked Mrs. Carpenter, "were you entitled to white at your wedding?"

"Well..." There was a grin in the 92-year-old eyes. "Off-white?"

DURING the summer months the Madronna Community Club brings in ice cream every Saturday on the SS Lady Lucinda. It is packed in dry ice and sold right there on the wharf. Everybody has a chocolate-coated ice cream stick. It is the only ice cream most of us see.

One Saturday last summer I was eating an ice-cream stick when I felt a gentle tug on my sleeve. I looked down—not very far down—and there were the great pleading eyes of Mal. Mal is an enormous malamute dog who is the only companion of Silby, a very shy little man who lives in an old log cabin on one of the mountains.

Mal's being there meant that Silby was hiding in the bushes until all the islanders were gone and he could slip into the store—purposely left unoccupied for him by the Carpenters. He would put the money for his last week's purchases on the counter, and take his this week's purchases, listing them in his account book so Mr. Carpenter could later fill in the prices and make up the bill, and then he would slip away, with Mal at his heel.

After that I bought two ice-cream sticks each Saturday and Mal would always be there, with his polite little nudge on my elbow, to claim one. He was almost as shy as his master, but if I sat down on a wharf piling, he would put his head on my lap. It was such a big head that it more than filled my lap and used up half the lap of one of the children cuddled up on the adjoining piling. The children liked to have that great wolf's head so confidingly close.

When Mal and his master first came to Madronna they seemed to have nothing to live upon except the money Silby made by making furniture. On his first lonely visit to the store he put up a sign. If you wanted—say—a Cape Cod chair, you would write a note and pin it to the sign. The next week the chair would be on the store porch, and you would leave the money for it on the store counter. Nobody ever met Silby properly except young Charlie Jo.

Charlie went up to the log cabin once, and in, and sat down on one of the two chairs in the living room. Mal came to him first, threateningly, but eventually sat down beside him and leaned his big head against Charlie's arm. After about an hour Silby crept out of the kitchen and took the second chair. They sat for about another hour before Silby spoke, and they never did talk much. But after that Silby started to make wooden musical instruments for Charlie's band, and for customers that the band found for him when they performed on other islands or the mainland.

Last Saturday Mal was executed. It was according to the law of the island. Mr. Cuthbert found him eating a sheep he had killed. It was the third sheep that had been killed, and there are no wolves on this island. Only Mal. Mr. Cuthbert shot him.

Nobody blamed Mr. Cuthbert, a man has to protect the means by which he feeds his family. But it was a sad gathering in the store that day. Most of the islanders value dogs, and Mal was special. He was Silby's whole family. Silby, the wispy little man of whom most of us have caught only glimpses as he dodges through the trees. Silby, who didn't have much, probably not enough to feed a big dog like Mal.

When Charlie Jo came in and heard, he didn't blame Mr. Cuthbert either. He just went out to find Silby where he would be hiding in the bushes, waiting for us to go and Mal to come.

DID you ever notice how the right-thinking young do what they think is right, and then are pained when they find that the adults whom they have drafted without consent object to carrying the main burden?

Charlie Jo is a very kind young person—18 going on 19—and he was distressed when Silby lost his malamute dog. Charlie stayed with Silby until the first shock was over, and then went out in his boat to ask his Indian relatives to put the word up the coast that he needed two identical malamute pups. He refrained from mentioning it until the pups had arrived and the first had been tucked into Silby's arms.

Then he brought the second to me.

I did NOT want a second dog. Especially a pup that would eat more meat than the rest of the family put together and get shot for chasing sheep or deer as soon as we had grown to love him.

After I had blown up, Charlie answered the last objection first. "Nobody'll shoot either of them. They won't know which is which. And nobody'll take the chance of shooting *your* dog—a woman alone with three little kids that need protection."

"They will if they're caught chasing sheep," I pointed out, ignoring the aspersion on my abilities. The men on the island have fixed ideas about protecting females and their young and since it extends, among other things, to keeping us in firewood, I do not go all over women's lib. But they won't have their sheep killed.

"Elwy Danson will break them of chasing sheep," said Charlie. Unanswerably. No dog trained by Elwy ever chases sheep again.

The pup by this time was exploring and Tippy, our dog,

was giving him the bared teeth. Tiger the cat, who is kind to the young of any species, sent Tippy yelping with a flick of her claws.

"Tiger will look after him," said Charlie complacently.

"She won't feed him."

"Mildred Stonehenge will shoot deer for both of them," said Charlie, "and old Robbie will catch them fish."

"Have you asked them?"

"Not yet. But they will. You could call him Wolf."

He looks like a wolf cub, except that his plumey tail curls around in a perfect circle and makes a nest for itself in the fur of his back. The wolves I've met wear their tails straight.

Mrs. Carpenter, bearing a 50-pound sack of dog chow, rowed over that evening to commiserate. The island, she reported, was taking its orders. Cursing Charlie, who had gone off with his rock band. The two pups will grow to about 90 pounds each.

We looked at the zoo, not a member of which I asked for. Well, Susie the mouse grew on us, I guess. But Coonie the three-legged raccoon was there already, the Carpenters decided we needed Tippy, the two cats just moved in, The Macaw is staying till Charlie's current girl friend leaves, and even Narce the peacock has snuck back (Caw drove him home to the Cuthberts) because he loves our mirrors. But he's using the upstairs mirrors till Caw goes.

"One thing Charlie forgot," said Mrs. Carpenter. "Once they're grown those two malamutes would be on every female dog in the island."

Like Charlie, Mrs. Carpenter acts before she announces. Charlie and the other island males don't know it, but those two pups are going to lose their manhood.

GOOD things last. This stubborn human belief, despite massive evidence to the contrary, gave Madronna Island a very busy Christmas weekend.

It had been the mildest autumn in anybody's memory so everybody assumed that it was going to go on being mild. No houses had been winterized.

Christmas Eve it snowed and then froze. Solid.

Mr. Carpenter and Richard James and Elwy Danson and Charlie Jo put the island's only chains on the government truck, making it the island's only mobile vehicle, and spent Christmas Eve and Christmas Day fending off disasters.

They drained trucks and cats for absent loggers. They helped old Robbie Robinson get his boat on the slip, because the fresh-water creek it was riding in was freezing and could crack its hull. They shut off the water to summer cottages and holiday-emptied homes, drained water systems and closed doors and windows—people never learn, although Madronna's resident thief, Captain O'Grady, is always ready to teach them. They rescued Elinor Filibruster's husband from Elinor. He had not prepared their house for frost, the pipes had burst and the kitchen was flooded.

Richard locked Elinor in the living-room and turned up the radio. Then the rest of them repaired the damage with the plumbing tools they had brought along, swept the worst of the water out the back door and took Elinor's husband along with them.

As Mr. Carpenter put it, the poor chap would be safer that way.

They took Mrs. Carpenter and Mrs. Carpenter's collection of skates and all the island children and mothers to the slough, which only freezes enough for skating about three days one year in four. (I do believe there were some children who did not get around to opening their Christmas presents until Tuesday, because you can't waste good skating weather.)

They saw a blaze on the horizon and found old Jarge Gallagher fighting a chimney fire. Actually, it had spread to the roof, and they only got it out by putting Richard—the lightest present—on the roof and passing buckets of snow up to him. He got the fire out eventually, but then he fell through the roof (they had also been passing up some of Captain O'Grady's gin). They mended the roof. Then they picked up the skaters and Elinor and delivered them to various places for Christmas dinner—that was around midnight, and got back to the store to find an hysterical Tony Beliski.

Tony is one of the small loggers who move around the islands taking off isolated lots of timber. When a logger brings a cat on the island, he is supposed to put up a bond with Mr. Carpenter for any damage the cat may do to island trails. Tony had saved the bond by sneaking the cat ashore from a barge.

Mr. Carpenter had therefore not known about it and had therefore not drained it and it was therefore probably a cat with a cracked block. A cat, that is, worth $28,000, not paid for, and suitable only for retirement to Jarge's rest home for old machinery.

They were still trying to comfort Tony with Captain O'Grady's gin when the Captain himself turned up. The Captain had known about the illegal transfer of the cat to Madronna, having observed it while illegally removing some logs from a passing broom, and had very kindly gone along with his boat, found the cat where it was hidden in the bush, drained and saved it.

Peace on earth.

I RWIN Hoffstater is always building a boat. He may have had some training before he came to Madronna—his memory is unreliable—or he may just have a knack for it. Irwin's boats are surprisingly seaworthy.

He gets the lumber for them by delivering logs to the Cooper Island mill, receiving in return half the finished planks in designated sizes. The Cooper mill gets the work because it has a planer. The ribs of Irwin's boats are made of Madronna oak. These he cuts and sands and shapes himself in a steam hut old Les Chumley let him build by the creek behind his shack.

When a boat is finished, Irwin gives it to somebody who needs a boat, and starts building another.

It was Mr. Carpenter who instituted the giving part. The first time Irwin built a boat he sold it and went to town and got, as usual, rolled and beaten. So Mr. Carpenter said, no more sales. And now Irwin gives them away, and the people who receive them are supposed to supply him with clothes and fishing tackle and tools and other necessities, and they mostly do—or if they don't, Mrs. Carpenter has a word with them.

There is one other problem with his boats. When a boat is reaching the point where it needs an engine, the island has to keep a close eye on Irwin. As a general rule he does not steal, but when he has a boat that needs an engine, he will do anything to get the money to buy the engine.

In fact, Mr. Carpenter is afraid that the $500 lost by one of the island's pensioners—a well-heeled pensioner, Mr. Carpenter is glad to say—went to buy an engine for one of Irwin's boats. The $500 was behind a picture on the pensioner's wall (instead of in Mr. Carpenter's drawer where it would have been safe), and the week after it went missing Irwin had an engine for his new boat.

The way Mr. Carpenter handles it now, when possible, is to designate the recipient of the boat well ahead of time and get him to buy the engine.

We will not have to worry about the engine for Irwin's current boat for a while.

Some time ago Richard James, our resident freelance writer, was appalled to discover that none of the children knew who Goliath was. They didn't know who David was, for that matter, or at any rate *that* David. Richard, like Mr. Carpenter and Charlie Jo, claims to be an agnostic; but he holds that one cannot be well grounded in English literature without a sound knowledge of the Bible (King James version) and Shakespeare. He is doing the Bible first. Mrs. Gathercole, the teacher, lets him take the children at the schoolhouse after regular school hours, provided he banks the fire before he leaves. He reads the Bible stories.

Irwin can't read but he loves stories. So he has been turning up every afternoon since the project began. One of the earliest stories was about Noah. The next morning Irwin began to lay the slip for the Ark.

The Ark was a three-story vessel, 300 cubits long, 50 cubits wide and 30 cubits high. A cubit, Richard explained to Irwin, was 18 to 20 inches. They decided that 18 inches would be the most suitable measurement for Madronna's Ark because the Cooper mill turns out lumber by the foot.

Irwin has been busy on the Ark ever since but, as Richard says, it will probably be several years before we have to worry about his sinking a passing merchantman to get an engine for her.

THE purpose of Brother John's visit to the Joes' is to persuade Charlie Jo to enter university next fall. He has no idea what incidental benefits he has bestowed.

The first was to get rid of Charlie Jo's current girlfriend. Brother John has no notion of this, but as soon as the girlfriend heard that he was moving in she moved out. She said she couldn't go on living in sin with Charlie if the Church was going to be in the next room. Mrs. Carpenter says that was just the chit's excuse, that she had decided she couldn't detach Charlie from his family, his rock band or Madronna Island and was just getting out, and good for her. (Mrs. Carpenter has been ambivalent about the chit; she can't stand her, she loves Charlie, but she won't disguise from her conscience that Charlie has been what she considers a Bad Boy.)

The second benefit was that the chit's departure (the whole island saw her off with much relief) made it possible for Charlie to reclaim The Macaw. The chit had made it clear that it was either her or The Macaw. So the Macaw has been staying with us.

Caw is a good enough bird, but he has declined to be one of the family. He has made it plain that while we will do to be getting on with, the only acceptable person in his universe is Charlie. He has been a visitor, and a captious, quarrelsome, noisy visitor, with an absolute genius for getting goats.

He drove Narce the peacock out of the house to begin with and then reduced him to skulking around the upstairs mirrors. Every night he has battled Coonie the three-legged raccoon for the kitchen rocking chair. He has taken it out on the two dogs and one of the cats. He has persisted in stealing the tiny wooden Buddha which Tiger,

175

the other cat, stole from the Carpenters, and every time she came back from hunting she had to take it away from him.

Then there's the phone. Our party line ring is one short and two longs, and Caw learned it in no time. He also learned that he got interesting results if, after imitating the ring, he called up the stairs in either Michael or Judy's voice, "Muh-muh! Tel-e-phone!"

He likes best to do it somewhere between 3 and 4 a.m.

He knew the instant Charlie arrived that he was going home. Like a flash he was off the back of the rocker and on Charlie's shoulder, gabbling in his ear, stroking his cheek with his bill and generally indicating that he'd be just as glad to go as we would be to see him go. Then he remembered the Buddha, went to claim it from the mantelpiece (Tiger was out hunting) and returned to Charlie's shoulder with the Buddha in his left claw.

They were just leaving when Tiger returned.

She got the picture at once, swarmed up Charlie to reclaim her Buddha, ran into more resistance than usual, and got it back with the spilling of quite a lot of blood. All Charlie's. The chit ought to know that it was another female that used him for a battleground.

But you have to admire Charlie. He stood absolutely still for a moment and then stepped over to the kitchen mirror and studied his face. "I'll have to get Mrs. Carpenter to make me a mask," he said, as I brought out the bandaids. "We've got to use Brother John on the grouse drums while we've got him."

That's the other benefit Brother John doesn't know he's going to be dispensing. He's an accomplished drummer, and he's going to be introducing Silby of Madronna's grouse drums to the world.

BROTHER John was getting a lesson on the grouse drums created by Silby of Madronna. Silby was hiding in the bedroom off the Carpenters' kitchen to hear but not be seen. Mrs. Carpenter was making a mask to cover the wounds inflicted on Charlie Jo by our cat Tiger in reclaiming her Buddha (I haven't the space to explain). And Charlie Jo was not hearing Brother John's pitch to recruit him for university next fall.

"You have an IQ of 153," Brother John told Charlie. "You have leadership qualities. You have an engaging personality. It is your duty to prepare yourself for a position of leadership among your people."

"You're still taking it fast," said Charlie (of Brother John's drumming, not his speech). "Listen to one stroke. It takes longer to complete its sound than a stroke on an ordinary drum."

It did, too. The drums consist of deep thigh pads, made of heavy drill and stuffed with goose down. The sticks are sort of mitts, only big like almost-inflated footballs and made of goose down-stuffed leather. Silby tried bull, calf, deer and moose leather before he got the effect he thinks he wants. The sound, when Brother John beats his thighs, is that of a grouse drumming out his springtime affections. Extremely big but a soft sort of bigness, more whoom than boom, and lingering.

"He leads here," said Mr. Carpenter, through the last of the lingering.

"Yes, I know, Mr. Carpenter," said Brother John. "But his capacities are needed in a much larger arena."

"You'll be in one with him tonight," said Mrs. Carpenter.

"An entertainment arena," said Brother John,

whooming again. "It's in the social and political arenas that his people need leaders."

"You just take it very slow like that," said Charlie, "and the rest of us will play around you. We're going to drive the pedal-car on the stage, so Silby can lie in the bottom and hear without being seen. He's shy, but he has to hear because the drums are still experimental."

"That pedal-car won't carry seven of us, it'll blow a tire," said Brother John, whooming very slowly.

"If it does, the others will change it, with great dignity and balefulness. And you will beat your drums with great dignity and balefulness. It doesn't matter what we do, so long as we're dignified and baleful."

"Why?"

"Because we're witches and warlocks."

"Why are we witches and warlocks?"

"Because Mrs. Carpenter made our costumes from a bale of undertaker's fabric. Also, it covers any deficiencies in our performance."

"Charlie, Charlie," said Brother John, "to waste such abilities!"

But he was whooming in a slow, dignified and baleful way as they prepared to set off for the SS Lady Lucinda. With Brother John and Charlie Jo being warlocks on the back of the plastic pedal-car, Silby lying on their feet, two witches sitting cross-legged behind the bucket seats and two warlocks pedalling.

"A plastic pedal-car and witchcraft!" said Brother John. "This is ridiculous."

"Ironic," said Charlie Jo.

"I guess I taught you," sighed Brother John, and went on whooming.

Charlie Jo will get Brother John to the concert, but it will be a question of fascinating interest to Madronna whether Brother John gets Charlie Jo to university.

AS Richard James explained to Mrs. Carpenter and me, sitting in the SS Lady Lucinda on the way to the mainland, it isn't talking the ethical life that presents the problems, it's living it.

"Ha!" said Mrs. Carpenter.

"There's so much moral blackmail," said Richard. "Sandra is in the hold with her kittens." Sandra was named after Richard's second to latest (not last) common-law wife. "I am taking Sandra to the vet's to have her removed from the production line, and the kittens to a pet shop I've discovered which will guarantee to find them good homes for $2 a head."

Richard, who is an agnostic, has been taking the children in Bible readings (the King James version being an essential, he holds, to a sound basis in English). But nothing ever stops where it starts. From the King James version they got, via the Golden Rule, to kindness to animals and a delegation of children bearing a starved and pregnant cat to Richard's houseboat.

She ate him out of house and home, got him under her paw and then (not yet trusting even her own human) retreated to a secret spot on Madronna to have her kittens. She turned up regularly for meals, but all four of them had their eyes open before she carried them back up the gangplank. Two orange. Two black and white.

As a public adherent of kindness to animals Richard could not, of course, take advantage of the island's execution chamber (Doe Kelly's gasoline washing machine exhaust with a plastic bag taped to its end). It had cost him a fortune in telephone calls, reported Les Chumley who listened in on all of them, to find a shop which would place them, for a fee, in happy homes.

"And I shall insist on a list of the homes with phone numbers so I can check back," said Richard. "Being commerical types they are no doubt capable of taking my $8 and sending them to the Humane for destruction."

But when we met him that night he shook three 20-dollar bills in our faces. *"They,"* he said, "paid *me.*"

"I thought they might," said Mrs. Carpenter.

"What do you mean, you thought they might?" demanded Richard.

"Well, anybody could have told," said Mrs. Carpenter. "Anybody," she added unkindly, "who knew the least thing about animals."

"You mean to say," said Richard, "that for the last six weeks you left me harboring…"

"It was perfectly safe so long as you didn't excite them," said Mrs. Carpenter.

"Excite what?" I asked.

"Two baby skunks," said Mrs. Carpenter and Richard together. "The black and white ones were not kittens," explained Richard to me, "they were skunks. At any moment they could have made my houseboat uninhabitable. And this woman…"

"You were much safer not knowing," said Mrs. Carpenter.

"The shop is going to have them descented," said Richard, turning from horror, "and expects to get as much as $150 for each of them. Cast thy kits upon the water (if I may freely translate the King James version): for thou shalt find them skunks worth $30 apiece after many days. I must draw it to the attention of the children. I wonder how Sandra detached them from their mother. But"… with renewed horror… "if she is going to keep this kind of company…"

"You needn't worry," said Mrs. Carpenter kindly, "unless they start to walk on their front feet with their hind feet in the air."

ITS been just the last two days we've known for sure that Anna Peterson was going. She won't let Doc Filbert call the ambulance boat to take her to hospital. "I'll die in my time and God's time," she told him. "They'll not hitch me to one of those machines."

She sits in one of the two over-stuffed chairs in the living-room of the tiny house Jed built when they retired. She can no longer get her breath lying down. Jed works in the flower garden she can see from her chair, and comes in every 15 or 20 minutes to tell her what he is doing. Over there he has put the gladiolas (which she will never see) and here the mignonette (whose sweet night scent she will never smell).

There is always a neighbor casually by, for Jed's heart will not admit what the doctor has told him. And for Jed Anna is merry still. It was when he had left, this morning, to go back to her garden, that she motioned me to the stool at her feet and took my hand.

"You have known grief, child?" she asked, and then, not waiting, "Yes, yes, we knew. The island knew. We didn't say , but we knew. When your husband died. And you came here with the three little children. And you always smiled. For the children. If you can't be happy, be as happy as you can. But you don't cry nights now, when the children are gone to sleep?"

"No."

She held my hand and fought for breath. We watched Jed working the earth around the begonias. "Will you tell him the timetable of grief when I'm gone?" she asked.

"Yes," I said.

"He's a doing man, my Jed," she said. "A fine carpenter. He'll make my coffin. But not a thinking man. It

181

will help him to know the way grief goes. And that it does go. And that I wanted him to know. I've always been around before to jolly him out of troubles."

She was a long time silent.

"Tell him the first three-four months, it'll be agony. His heart will hurt. Real physical hurt. All the time. His mind will be always coming back to the thought of me dead. His back will bend. You'll not be able to reach him."

A long , long pause.

"See he gets lots of the Captain's gin."

A pause.

"But then life'll trick him. Charlie Jo'll say something funny and he'll laugh. He'll be that ashamed. He'll go into the back bedroom and cry. The hurt'll be worse than ever."

For almost 30 seconds she seemed not to breathe.

"Life'll trick him again and again. He'll notice the second blooming of the dogwood, and be ashamed. He'll hear the wild geese honking south, and be ashamed."

This time it seemed a minute before she breathed again.

"After a year...you tell him all of this...it'll not be so bad. He'll not be able to look back and say, 'this time last year Anna and me...'

"After two years he'll wake up one day and not remember me at all. He'll whistle putting butter on his porridge. The porridge will taste good...It'll be maybe three-four days before he remembers he's forgotten me..."

"And that will be the saddest time of all," I said gently.

"Yes. But that you'll not tell him. My Jed's not a thinking man. If that last bit's not put in words, he'll feel the hurt, but it will pass the quicker. It will all pass..."

We watched while Jed set a jar of honeysuckle by the window, to tempt the humming birds for her to see.

WHEN the big winds blow, souls on a light line slip away.

When the wind that evening got bad, I left the children with Irwin Hoffstater and climbed the mountain to the tiny house where old Anna Peterson is dying so cheerfully that her husband, Jed, can make himself believe that she is not. But he was alarmed now and had called Doctor Filbert who had phoned for Sergeant Munro and the ambulance boat.

"I can't give you hope, Jed," the doctor was saying when I got there. "She's known she was going and she knows now she's going tonight."

The Carpenters came then. Jim Carpenter had been out in the government truck with Richard James, making sure that the islanders were under cover where they couldn't be hit by trees. But they knew where the need was greatest.

"What we've got to do," the doctor told us, "is help her go out quietly. Carpenter, you and Richard, you've been helping the islanders. Tell us about it. The funny bits. If I know Anna, she'll want to use the last of her breath on a laugh."

We went into the little living-room then, where Anna was sitting in a chesterfield chair—she could no longer get her breath lying down—and Mrs. Carpenter was perched on the side of it with an arm around her. I sat by Anna's feet, where she could feel me. As death creeps up the touch of a human body can help.

It was a hard night, but not ghoulish. Richard and Mr. Carpenter, talking easily—really easily, whatever it cost them—told us about their adventures. And Anna did laugh, gasping, when they told how they had tied up Elinor Filibruster and taken her down to Irwin and the children. We none of us much like Elinor. "And if that big old fir she insisted on keeping goes,'' said Mr. Carpenter, ''it'll take not only their cottage but the whole point.''

One thing which gave a sad reality to what we all knew was not real was that Jed could not believe she was dying.

He kept going into the kitchen to watch for the boat. ''The Sergeant'll have you to hospital in no time,'' he'd come back and tell Anna. ''And while you're off I'll get the new linoleum laid in the kitchen. You still want red?''

''Yes, red,'' gasped Anna.

After a while there was a bang on the door, and it was young Charlie Jo. ''Just came up to watch from the kitchen for the Sergeant's boat,'' he explained. ''I'll catch his lines.'' Charlie's arrival meant that the whole of Madronna was sitting up, this night, with Anna and Jed. Someone had listened to the doctor's call on the party line, and put out the word.

It was hard to tell when she died. The breaths would stop, for maybe a minute or two, and we would think, she is gone. But then, with a kind of convulsion, there would be another breath. It was when the last silence had lasted a long time that we were sure.

But Jed wouldn't believe it. He would go to her and kiss her. He would push up her fallen jaw and kiss her on the mouth. He would promise that when she got back from hospital the red linoleum would be on the kitchen floor. He would say, ''We'll need the Sergeant. He'll help to carry you down the mountain.''

It was Charlie Jo who broke through the old man's determined dream. He came out of the kitchen and put his arm around Jed. ''Yes,'' he said, ''we'll need the Sergeant. But first, sir, you'll have to come and help me make her coffin.''

The old man cried out a terrible cry then, louder than the sea and wind. He rocked back and forth in agony, and the boy's arm held him. He was crying still when they went out the door together, not looking back at Anna in her chair, to go to the workshop and start steaming the wood for her coffin.

Y OUNG Charlie Jo is the only person on Madronna who knows anything about Silby, but that isn't to say *knows*. They have exchanged maybe ten or eleven sentences, Charlie says, and they have sat on either side of Silby's table for several hours on a couple of occasions, communicating on some other wave length, but even with Charlie Silby goes to extreme lengths not to be seen or heard. When Charlie takes an order up the mountain for one of Silby's hand-made musical instruments, he writes it on a piece of paper and puts in under a rock beside the door of Silby's cabin. And although Charlie can usually hear him rustling a bit inside, he never comes out to get the paper until Charlie's gone.

So Silby was well into pneumonia before Charlie, having gone up two days running and heard no rustling, went inside and found him. He carried Silby, in his sleeping bag, down to our place, right through our midst and up to the back bedroom over the kitchen, which is the warmest. With Mal, Silby's malamute pup, at his heels.

"I'd have taken him to the Carpenters'," said Charlie, coming down and ringing for Doc Filbert on the party line, "but I thought he'd be less scared of the children. Can you fill some hot water bottles while I talk to the Doc?"

The doctor came over, refused to diagnose a patient from behind a closed door, pumped Silby full of antibiotics, came down to announce that we probably couldn't save him, said he'd be back in four hours, and that on no account was anybody but Charlie or young Michael to go into the nut's room. "He'd rather meet his maker than you or Mrs. Carpenter," said the Doc, departing.

He sent Mrs. Carpenter over, however, and the nursing was carried on by Charlie and Michael, with instructions from below. Mal, the pup, wouldn't come out and wouldn't eat either. Charlie reported that he was inside Silby's sleeping bag, with his head on Silby's right shoulder. After Michael's first visit, Blackie the cat was inside the sleeping bag on the other side, with his head cuddled in Silby's neck and one black paw on Silby's cheek.

"He kind of pats him now and then," reported Michael. "Silby took half the orange juice."

Mrs. Carpenter showed Charlie and Michael how to put a bedpan under a helpless patient. They had to handle it in turns, because it went on for three days and three nights. The pup never did come out, but Charlie and Michael got some water into his mouth with an invalid feeder. After the first time, Mrs. Carpenter made them use one feeder for Silby and another for the dog, although the Doc scoffed. "Fine healthy dog," he said. "But perhaps you'd better. The nut might give him distemper."

Blackie the cat came out once for milk and once for hamburger.

The doctor insisted on staying in the room when the crisis was approaching, but Charlie made him sit on the floor where Silby couldn't see him.

When they came down we could tell by their faces that Silby had made it. Besides, the pup was with them. He ate all the animals' dishes empty before I could get him one of this own. He was finishing up on some cream when Michael, who'd been wakened to sit by the invalid, came down the stairs.

"Silby wants some wood to make a whistle," he said.

"Well," said the Doc professionally, "he can have some wood to hold. But he can't start whittling till tomorrow."

T HE bedroom above the kitchen is at present out of bounds for everybody except the children and Charlie Jo. It is occupied by Silby, our reclusive musician and maker of musical instruments, who is recovering from pneumonia and is afraid of all grownups except Charlie. Doc Filbert says Silby needs feeding up. "You better keep him for three weeks ... a month. The children can carry his trays. I'll send Mrs. Carpenter over to shout him into the bathroom for a bath. But you better draw the bath first. He wouldn't know how."

So the Doc departs and Mrs. Carpenter comes over and sits on the stairs and shouts Silby into the bathroom. "And I'll examine the ring on the tub to make sure you took the bath," she bellows.

We convene over coffee in the kitchen. The house is by no means invalid-quiet. It hasn't been since the day after Silby passed the crisis, when he sent Charlie Jo up to his shack on the mountain to bring back his inventory of musical instruments. Charlie then took off with his rock band, and Silby has since been undermining him with the children. He is teaching them jazz.

At least, that is what Richard James says is beginning to come out of the bedroom above the kitchen. "What does he say it is?" Richard asks my son Michael, who is beating it up the stairs—post bath—with half the rest of the school at his heels.

"He doesn't *say* anything," replies Michael, not pausing. "He just blows and then we blow."

There are eight of them up there with Silby and they are all blowing. First Silby on each of eight different instruments, and then each of the children, and then all nine of them (we presume) together. "Really remarkable,"

187

says Richard, reaching out to turn up the radio to give the kitchen its own sound sanctuary.

"Mum, *please!*" calls my daughter Judy from the upstairs landing.

We turn down the radio.

"I wouldn't put up with it," says Elinor Filibruster, who has dropped in to find the worst. "If he needs nursing, call the ambulance boat and send him to town."

"I brought you some chick peas," said Mrs. Carpenter. "There's always chick peas on the order he leaves on the store counter when we're out."

A fine flourish from upstairs, amazingly only slightly discordant. Or maybe the discords are intended.

"He wrote it down for Michael," I explain. "Chick peas, chopped potatoes, chopped onions—in tomato soup. He's a vegetarian."

"How do you know?" demands Elinor.

"I don't know. But Charlie says he never eats any of the deer meat Mildred Stonehenge shoots for his pup. And listen to those animals."

We listen. The jazz band has four animal members. Tippy the dog barking. Blackie the cat occasionally but not always (being a cat he has to preserve his independence) yowling. The two malamute pups howling (apparently malamutes can't bark).

Tiger the cat, who is preserving her independence by remaining below, decides to get rid of Elinor by jumping in her lap. Elinor can't stand cats and departs, repeating, "I wouldn't put up with it. Just a sheer collapse of discipline."

Meaning my discipline. We listen to the cacophony upstairs.

"Well at least," says Mrs. Carpenter, "you know where they are."

We do. Indeed we do.

I T'S about my brother," offered Loretta Cuthbert, 11, sitting uneasily on the edge of Coonie's rocker in the kitchen. Loretta is one of the people Coonie allows to use his rocker.

"Yes?" I said.

Long pause.

"He's feeling pretty bad. He's up in the field with Jenny and Timson. He wouldn't come to the jazz band practice." Jenny is the Cuthberts' Clydesdale mare and Timson is her fox terrier friend; 12-year-old Johnny Cuthbert is viewed with approval by both of them; and the jazz band has been practicing in the bedroom above my kitchen ever since Silby, Madronna's musical recluse, began his recovery from pneumonia (children and animals welcome, no adults allowed).

Johnny ought to have been upstairs blowing something. He wasn't.

"Why is he feeling bad?" I asked.

"Because the bishop says he has to be christened, and my Mum and Dad said okay. In the church on Sunday," expanded Loretta in a burst, "and only the Elsons' baby will be christened too and all the kids will be sitting in the front because the bishop makes them and Johnny'll have to stand up there and have water put on him and the kids'll laugh and he can't bear it."

"I see," I said. I did see.

The bishop has not been tactful. Knowing nothing about Madronna, including the fact that Madronna was building a non-denominational chapel, he put a prefab church here. The money was provided by a Toronto parish, which injured local pride. Local pride somewhat re-established itself by auctioning the church's furnishings off to islanders, sending the money to the Toronto parish for its mission fund, and recapturing from the bishop's church on Cooper Island certain sacred silver that had been willed to Madronna. Satisfactory, in its way. But Charlie Jo had best served local pride.

Sending out an emergency call through the Indian fishing fleet he got quick delivery of an evangelist who baptized all Madronna's youth in Clare Creek before the bishop could lay a hand on. Except Johnny, who was away. Johnny hadn't been done. So the bishop was going to do him now. In the face of all his contemporaries and in the company of an infant. Not tactful.

"Let me think," I said to Loretta.

While I thought, Coonie the three-legged coon came in the window and got on the back of his rocking chair. Loretta toasted a piece of brown bread, buttered and honeyed it and handed it to Coonie. He offered Loretta a corner of toast. She took it. They sat munching and rocking together. I remembered that when I'd been a probationer nurse (I never got past the probation) a lecturer in nursing ethics had explained that any person who had herself been christened could, in an emergency, christen another.

I remembered that when little sisters take their brothers' troubles to a strange adult, the troubles are real.

"Let's go," I said.

Johnny sat drooping in the Cuthberts' back meadow. Jenny the horse had her big head on his shoulder. The paws of Timson the terrier clasped his foot.

Later on I let myself into the church and entered the details in the church record. Christened: John Cuthbert. Godmother, Jenny Cuthbert. Godfather, Timson Cuthbert. Font .. well, we needn't mention the horse trough.

Tonight I'll phone the bishop and tell him. The bishop will disapprove.

But he isn't the final Authority.

CAPTAIN O'Grady saw it first. He was studying this passing log-boom with his binoculars, undoubtedly to discover if it had been carelessly boomed so that under cover of darkness he could take his boat alongside and steal some of the logs, when he saw something peculiar. Charlie Jo was working on the rock band's plastic pedal car at the wharf, so the Captain took him as crew and they went out to the log-boom.

While the Captain held his boat to the boom with a pike-pole, Charlie went to look at the peculiar thing and the tug-boat crew raised hell on their loudhailer. They know the Captain. What Charlie found was an emaciated dead female cougar and two cougar kittens, one of them still alive. He and the captain brought the live one to me.

The ewes are throwing a lot of twin lambs this year and quite often they will only feed one. So Mrs. Carpenter and Mrs. Cuthbert are both bottle-feeding three rejected lambs and I am bottle-feeding one. The Captain and Charlie therefore decided that I was the natural for cougar raising.

I was so mad I kicked the milkcan across the kitchen and its lid came off and there was milk all over the floor and Charlie had to go up to the Cuthberts' to get it filled again.

It is a mistake to get a reputation for being kind to animals.

It isn't the zoo aspect I mind. When you have a dog, two malamute pups, a peacock, two cats, a pet mouse, a visiting two-year-old deer, a visiting three-legged coon, a lamb, and a musical recluse attracting half the island's children to play jazz in the bedroom above the kitchen, it's a zoo you have on your hands, and only a slattern could exist in the middle of it. But I am a slattern and the island knows it. Doc Kelly comes faithfully to clean up the worst of it. What bothers me is that you can't be kind to wild animals, not really.

Big Boy the deer will be shot some hunting season because we have let him believe that humans are friends. The baby cougar will grow up to be a big cougar, and if he stays on Madronna he will kill sheep and deer and somebody will shoot him, and anyway he won't have a mate. There are no other cougars on Madronna.

"I'll teach him to hunt," offered Charlie against my raging, "and when he's grown I'll take him to the mainland and release him in a wild place where he'll find his own people."

"Silby says he'll do the night feedings for you, Mum," said five-year-old Dorene on behalf of the musical recluse who was too shy to come downstairs and say it himself.

"I think this milk is about right," said Captain O'Grady, sticking his finger in the milk he was warming on the kitchen stove.

Michael and Judy pushed me, still raging, into Coonie's rocking chair. Charlie laid the little cougar in my lap. Tiger the cat leaped on the rocking chair arm to establish maternal supervision over the new infant. The Captain handed me the bottle of warm milk. The lamb laid his nose on what he didn't know was an ancient enemy.

He was pretty far gone, poor wee thing. I had to shake milk on my finger and put it in his mouth several times before he got the idea, and even then he sucked weakly. But as the warm milk got inside him, he began to pull more strongly, and then greedily.

Right now he's asleep behind the kitchen stove, between Tiger and her other baby, the lamb.

I don't think The New Columbia Encyclopedia can have lived with malamutes before. It should know better for the next edition. It has just spent a couple of minutes on the floor with two of them and the children are now sitting at the other end of the kitchen table Scotch-taping 72 pages back in.

The New Columbia has lived on that end of the table ever since Richard James gave us a copy because he says it is essential to satisfy the curiosity of children. But not necessarily always by answering questions. "Tell them to look it up," he said. So Michael and Judy, the twins, do. And Dorene, who is just five, adds to the sticky finger-prints by standing on a chair and pretending to.

When Charlie Jo gave us our malamute pup Wolf (against my will but to serve as protection for the malamute pup, Mal, of Silby, our musical recluse), we looked up malamutes. "The malamute," said the New Columbia, "is by nature a gentle and devoted companion; claims of wolf ancestry have never been proved." Ha!

Devoted, yes. Gentle? Well, maybe, by wolf standards.

Mal as well as Wolf has been with us for the past month, while Silby recovered from pneumonia in the bedroom above the kitchen. They may have spurred each other on.

The first day they were together they forced open the food cupboards (which we keep locked on account of Coonie, the three-legged coon), and ate practically everything. Not the spices. They can't open my tins of home-canned salmon, but they can puncture them with their teeth and lie there sucking at them until we might as well do the opening for them. We have to keep the kerosene fridge roped because they opened and emptied that, too.

Another thing the New Columbia is temperate about is size. Mature malamutes, it says, weigh 70 to 85 pounds. These two pups are just five months old and they weigh 70 pounds apiece. Half the island has had to hunt and fish to keep them in grub.

But is was yesterday that we decided we had to take steps. One of them (the children say Mal and Silby says Wolf) came charging in from a frolic outdoors and took Judy's ankle in his mouth and was so affectionate that Doc Filbert had to put in six stitches. We are all convinced that Mal/Wolf simply didn't know his own strength. But Elwy Danson, who is the islander who knows how to train dogs, is on his way over to collect the two of them, Michael and Judy and Silby. He says Michael, Judy and Silby have to stay at his place till they've learned to control their dogs. I believe it's done with rolled-up newspapers and constant shouts of "No!"

It will be hard on Silby, who is so shy of adults that the only time I've seen him since he joined us was when Charlie Jo carried him through the kitchen and up the stairs to the back bedroom. Charlie and Michael did the nursing, and during his recuperation Silby has been giving jazz lessons to half the island children.

Elwy Danson will make him live with the family.

A voice just said from the stairs behind me, "Thank you, Missus, for all you've done for me." "You're welcome," I replied, not looking around. It's bad enough for Silby to have to be heard, let alone seen. He's sneaking out the front door now, with Mal at his heels, to wait for Elwy and at least a month of adult companionship.

What a man will do for his dog.

WHAT we like about the oil company that is drilling on Madronna is that it is rather unworldly about little things—little things to the oil company, that is.

It is paying union wages to Elwy Danson's logging crew and Thorn Robertson's sawmill crew to put up temporary housing for the oil crew, because it didn't send enough. (Madronna has no unions, but Richard James, our resident freelance journalist, had to make just one phone call to the mainland to find out what union rates are. Jed Peterson, who is a qualified carpenter, is getting carpenter rates.)

The oil crew and the Community Club decided where the extra housing would go and it isn't exactly extra housing. The crew (they are an obliging bunch) is going to double up in the portable housing the company sent, and Madronna is building them a club house on dry land behind Les Chumley's back meadow where they are going to drill for oil.

The club house is being built so that it will not be portable. It is being made of rough lumber from the island sawmill (delivered at mainland prices), and on the inside it will be finished with rough cedar also from the sawmill but planed by a portable planer Thorn Robertson rented from town.

It is going to be quite a nice club house; Thorn proposed a plate-glass front and the oil crew agreed; and there is already a brisk battle between Richard who wants it (post oil drilling) for a library and Elinor Filibruster who wants it for a hobby shop.

The oil crew hasn't started drilling yet because Les Chumley's back meadow isn't exactly a meadow; it's a bog. So the toolpusher, who is the oil crew foreman, has

195

hired Elwy Danson to fill the bog with rock. Elwy has rented three heavy-duty dump trucks and two loaders from town. Mr. Carpenter and Captain O'Grady are blasting rock off the side of a mountain, on the payroll, naturally, of the oil company. Mr. Carpenter has temporarily shelved his other job as government road foreman.

Madronna has even had to hire some extra hands from Cooper Island.

On the way home the other day I stopped to observe the bog-filling operation. It was informative. The trucks come down from the mountain bearing rock and dump it in the bog. Then they go over to the gravel pit on Mr. Carpenter's land and fill up with gravel (using the second loader) and dump it slowly on the road as they go back up the mountain. The government has never been willing to pay to have that road gravelled, but it can't handle such heavy traffic without. If filling the bog takes very long, Mr. Carpenter may get all the island trails gravelled. I guess you could say he hasn't entirely abandoned road making.

Because it may take quite a while to fill that bog.

I stopped Elwy Danson on his second trip with a load of rock and asked him about it. "Did anyone," I asked, viewing a bog that was gobbling rock but didn't seem to have any drainage although drainage was plainly possible, "tell the oil crew that water doesn't run up hill?"

There was a long pause.

"They didn't ask," said Elwy.

OUR first greenhorn of the season had to be rescued last Sunday.

We really weren't set up yet for rescues. Mrs. Carpenter and I were making white Kleenex roses for the wedding (which, as Mrs. Carpenter says, is a disgrace when Lily Island is shore to shore with real white lilies, but the bride wants white Kleenex roses). Michael was out fishing with Johnny Cuthbert in our respectable rowboat. The commercial boats were after herring. The non-commercial boats (at very commercial prices) were ferrying the oil crew here and there.

At which point Judy and Dorene presented themselves in the kitchen to announce, "There's a funny looking log out in the channel, Mum."

Brought into focus with the binoculars, the funny looking log turned out to be an upsidedown boat with a man lying on top of it.

I explained to Mrs. Carpenter about our unrespectable rowboat. It leaks and the single oar has a broken handle.

"You should always keep your boats in repair," said Mrs. Carpenter reprovingly. "Judy, get on the phone and try to round up a power boat. You may have to call Cooper Island. But try Elinor Filibruster first. She made Poor Pet go to church this morning, so he probably missed the oil crew. (Poor Pet is what Elinor calls her husband.) You'll bail," she told me.

The tide being with us, we got out to the craft—Mrs. Carpenter paddling with the broken oar, me bailing—in fairly quick time. The face peering at us from the upturned boat was very young, the spread-eagled body was in naval uniform. It got itself aboard our rowboat, babbling gratitude and remorse all over itself (its name was Rolf).

"Do you think you could take it in tow?" he babbled. "I took it without leave from the base on Cooper. Just for a sail, you know. And if I don't get it back they'll throw me out." Mrs. Carpenter took it in tow with our painter knotted to his painter.

They were paddling valiantly, Mrs. Carpenter with the broken oar, Rolf with a board; but I think we were going rather backwards (the tide now being against) when Elinor Filibruster and Poor Pet came alongside in their power boat. Poor Pet can be quite useful if somebody shouts Elinor down, which Mrs. Carpenter is always glad to do. He and Rolf had the sail boat upright in no time. Then he took the rowboat in tow and brought us all to our float.

Whereupon Elinor said that she would, of course, be putting in for salvage. "I think it's something like 50 per cent of the worth of the craft the salvager gets," she said. "The navy can afford it."

"But they'd throw Rolf out," said Mrs. Carpenter.

"Rolf should have thought of that," said Elinor.

Mrs. Carpenter looked thoughtful, Elinor looked triumphant, and Poor Pet and Rolf oozed despair. "Salvage," said Mrs. Carpenter then, "belongs to the first boat to get a line on the wreck. That was us."

"But... " said Elinor.

"That was us," said Mrs. Carpenter. "And the line's still on."

It was. And Elinor was still screaming when Poor Pet gunned up the motor and took her out of there.

We led the mariner up to the kitchen and dried him out before sending him back to base. He is coming over next weekend to pay salvage of a new pair of oars and a bottle of brandy for Poor Pet. Poor Pet can hide it in the woodshed.

OUR adopted baby cougar is now about three times the size of his foster mother, Tiger the cat. He still takes a bottle of milk whenever he can persuade somebody to offer him one, which is every three hours or so, but he has been graduated to small pieces of raw venison in between.

Charlie Jo had come up to tell me of the rock band's success on the mainland. He was hardly inside the door when Tiger decided to teach her cougar baby how to hunt. She had caught a mouse outside and brought it into the kitchen. She rubbed the squirming little thing against the kitten's nose. I got up immediately. What I always do when Tiger brings a mouse inside is pick her up, take her to the doorstep, shake her until she lets go and hold her—raucous with fury—until the mouse has escaped. This time Charlie Jo touched my arm. "No," he said.

Tiger laid the mouse at the cougar kitten's feet, and swatted the kitten to get his attention. The mouse started to run away. Tiger laid a paw on it and held it. She swatted the kitten again. She lifted her paw and let the mouse scurry an inch or two and brought the paw down again.

"That's enough of that," I said, starting for her, but Charlie grabbed my arm. "He has to learn to hunt," he said.

Tiger sank the claws of her right paw in the fur of the cougar kitten's forehead and pulled his face down. She lifted her left paw, the mouse scurried, the cougar kitten saw it and bumbled after it. Tiger caught it. She pressed it down with her paw, while the kitten nuzzled it. I shook off Charlie, but he edged between me and the animals.

"You eat. They eat," he said. "Tiger's a good mother. She's teaching her kitten what he has to do to live."

Tiger flipped the mouse across the floor with her paw,

and darted after and around it. She stood over its terror, while the kitten staggered toward her and brought his nose down on the mouse. He smelled. He did nothing else. Tiger gave the mouse a quick slash, drawing blood.

"Oh God," I said.

Charlie covered my eyes. "The kitten has got the idea," he said. "It'll be all right in a minute. There. He has caught it. He is mawling it a little. Now you can look. Tiger has killed it. She is showing him how to eat it." He removed his hands from my eyes.

Tiger was eating the mouse. She ate its head, while the cougar kitten nuzzled at the feast. Then she stood back and watched him eat the rest of it, the small grey body, the tail. Not quite all of the tail. Tiger washed the blood from his face.

"Shall I take the cougar kitten to Doe Kelly's execution chamber?" asked Charlie gently.

"No!"

"I could take him to my Grandmother. My Grandmother knows that all of us animals must learn to find their meat. But he wouldn't have Tiger to teach him."

"No. Go away. Just go away."

He went. He hadn't had any time to tell me about the rock band.

Tiger settled her cougar kitten in the warm place behind the stove, folding her paws around his head that was bigger, now, than hers. Her other baby, the lamb, crowded in to lie beside them.

I F you can't stand snakes, but have elected to live in a rural setting, you must immediately make it plain to the snakes that you are in charge. When sighting one, never scream, run away or permit children in the vicinity to perceive that you are afraid. The right approach to children who wish to bring a snake indoors is to explain that it would be unkind to separate him from his family and friends.

Elinor Filibruster has not fully adjusted to living on an island that has snakes.

At the moment, because Mrs. Carpenter wouldn't, I am giving Elinor lessons in driving a secondhand van she made her husband purchase. The lessons consist of driving round a more or less circle on a more or less level trail. The children were in the back, because we were going to drop them off at the shortcut to the Carpenters'. We got half way when we were stopped—Elinor screaming—by a snake curled up in the middle of the trail.

He declined to move.

I got down and viewed him. He was a boa constrictor (do not be alarmed, they come in all sizes) who had just had a meal. The meal was plainly visible as a bulge part way down his length. When I asked him politely to get off the trail, he hissed faintly.

Hunting around in the ditch I found a forked stick. While Elinor continued to scream—that woman has remarkable lungs—and the children observed with interest, I tried to hook the snake off the road, but he rose up like a hoop and rolled off. Apparently they go stiff when they are digesting; but he could still hiss. No, I didn't measure him, but the circle he made—and his head and tail overlapped—was about two feet in diameter.

After that I pushed Elinor, still screaming but now a little hoarse, out of the driver's seat and returned her and her van to Poor Pet, her husband. She was not equal to further instruction that day.

Not feeling all that equal myself (I am not sure that the snakes have assimilated the idea that I am in charge), I decided to go along with the children and seek comfort with the Carpenters.

On the way Judy sighted a lizard and Michael caught it. Obviously shaken momentarily out of a good line, I neglected to mention his family and friends, so they took him along, passing him from one to the other and even kindly offering me carrying privileges. I deferred to five-year-old Dorene, and the other two became taken up with teaching her the right way to carry a lizard.

Mrs. Carpenter always knows how to handle these things. She got an empty chocolate box, punched some breathing holes in it, and suggested they put Mac the lizard in it until they were ready to go home. They parked Mac in his box on the porch.

As soon as they were out of sight on the way down to the wharf with Irwin Hoffstater, I slipped out, lifted the chocolate box lid at one end, and hoped that Mac would escape.

He did.

When the children came back and found him gone, they were much distressed.

"We could have underestimated his strength," said Mrs. Carpenter. "He could have pushed up the lid." She had watched me pushing up the lid; she neither lies nor goes out to meet trouble. In time Mac might have pushed it up himself.

"But," said Michael sorrowfully, "we meant to take him back to his family and friends."